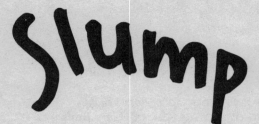

OTHER YEARLING BOOKS YOU WILL ENJOY:

YEARLING BOOKS are designed especially to entertain and enlighten young people. Patricia Reilly Giff, consultant to this series, received her bachelor's degree from Marymount College and a master's degree in history from St. John's University. She holds a Professional Diploma in Reading and a Doctorate of Humane Letters from Hofstra University. She was a teacher and reading consultant for many years, and is the author of numerous books for young readers.

Slump

a novel by

Dave Jarzyna

A YEARLING BOOK

by
...ing
an imprint of
Random House Children's Books
a division of Random House, Inc.
1540 Broadway
New York, New York 10036

Visit us on the Web! www.randomhouse.com/kids

Educators and librarians, for a variety of teaching tools, visit us at www.randomhouse.com/teachers

ISBN: 0-440-41514-4

Reprinted by arrangement with Delacorte Press

Printed in the United States of America

November 2000

10 9 8 7 6 5 4 3 2 1

OPM

To Annie and Ali
for their love;
to Susan for everything

1

I T WAS THE SAME dream—the one I'd had nearly every night for the past three weeks.

In the dream I'm sleeping on the couch, right there in front of the TV. All of a sudden I sit straight up, knowing I'm gonna be late.

So I panic.

I can't find my shoes, and no one's around to give me a ride. I jump on my bike, ride like a maniac, and finally get to school, all sweaty and tired and breathing real hard.

But the team's not there. So I start ripping through the halls looking for someone—anyone. Then, through the door leading outside, I see them out on the field. They're out there without me. Now I'm really mad, and I run out screaming, ready to rip somebody's head off.

When I finally get there, everybody stops—like somebody had just flipped a switch. A guy who I don't quite recognize turns and speaks so quietly that I can barely hear him.

"It's over, Evers," he says, almost in a whisper. "You missed it. Again."

But this time, at the point in the dream when everyone starts laughing at me, a blast of light suddenly pierced my brain. It was like someone rolled up the shade, letting a burst of sunshine into a dark attic.

"Geez," said the pixie voice of the person who was digging her fingers deep into my left eye socket, prying open my eyelid and making it very clear that I wasn't dreaming anymore. "Are you in a coma?"

"No," I grumbled at the creature hovering over me, my little sister, Shea. "I'm not in a coma, but I might put you in one."

"Oooh, big man," she said. "I think it's your Spider-Man sheets here that make you really scary. Now get up. Mom's been calling you for ten minutes."

"Lay off my sheets," I growled, pulling back my blanket. "At least *I* don't have Barbie sheets."

"But I'm nine," said Shea, shaking her short, shaggy brown hair out and away from her chocolate eyes. "You're a teenager. I don't think I'm gonna have Barbie sheets when I'm thirteen. Now get up."

When I didn't move, she turned and yelled toward the stairway, "Mom, Mitchie won't get up."

I threw off my blankets, pushed away the soccer ball that had somehow found its way on top of my bed, and stumbled to my feet. "I'm up, I'm up," I said, rubbing my eyes. Then I started moving toward Shea, dragging one foot behind me, my tongue hanging out and my arms spread wide. "Now come here, I want to give my baby sister a big, big hug."

She ran from my room screaming.

I staggered into the bathroom and raised my head

to look into the mirror. I have blond hair like my dad and blue eyes like my mom. I'm not real big, but I'm sturdy. My dad says I have the same big thighs and chest that his dad had, but I never saw him in person. He died before I was born.

I took my time making my way downstairs.

I walked into the kitchen. My mom was wiping the counter with one hand and combing Shea's hair with the other.

"Mitchell," Mom said. "Don't you need something from me? How are you for lunch money?"

"Don't worry about lunch. I'm thinking about going on a hunger strike."

"Ignore him, Mom," said the voice behind the sports page. My brother, Chuck, the star of the family.

"Mitchell," my mom continued, "you need to feed Shea tonight. Make some macaroni, and don't forget to throw some vegetables in the microwave."

"Can I throw them from the other end of the kitchen?" I asked.

"Don't worry, Mom," said Shea. "I'll handle it."

"I know you will, sweetheart," said my mom. "Mitchell, don't make your sister do *all* the work. Be ready to go at six-thirty. We're going to meet your father at the game, and I don't want to miss the player introductions. After all, it's the last game of the season."

"You're right, Mom," I said, flipping some frozen waffles into the toaster oven. "I sure don't want to miss seeing Chuck run onto the field, you know, with thousands of fans screaming and all the spastic girls yelling '*Chuck, ooooooh, Chuck!*' "

Chuck finally lowered the paper and gave me the eye. "What's with *you*?" he asked. "Something spook you during the night, or what?"

I shot him my tough-guy look, the one I practice in the mirror.

"Oh, come on, Mitchell," my mom said. "You love to watch Chuck's games."

"Well, of course I do," I shot back. "In fact, I *live* for Chuck's games."

And there was a time when that was true—even though it seemed like a lifetime ago.

My dad rushed into the kitchen. "Has anyone seen my keys?" he asked. His tie hung loose around his neck, and he looked stressed. He stopped and looked at me.

"Mitchie," he said. "I just walked by your room. I want all that junk off the floor before we go to the game tonight."

"Is that all, Dad?" I asked. "No 'Good morning, Mitchie'?"

"Don't start," he said. He didn't look happy. "We've only been asking you to get that mess cleaned up for the last month."

"Your keys are right where you left them," my mom told him, pointing to the kitchen counter.

He grabbed them. "I'll see everyone tonight. Don't forget, Mitchie."

"Sir, *yes sir*," I said under my breath as soon as he was out the door.

"Knock it off, Mitchell," said my mom. "You two have been sniping at each other for weeks now. You know he has a lot on his mind. It's not easy working full-time and going to school at night. Don't forget he's got that big test on Thursday."

"Yeah, that's right," I answered, not looking up. "The big test. How could I forget that?"

Within about thirty seconds Shea and my mom were gone and Chuck had raced out the door at the sound of his buddy Billy's car horn. And I was alone in the kitchen.

Again.

It's not that I minded being alone. Actually, I was getting very good at it.

Ever since my mom had gotten that job at the store by the mall selling carpet and curtains—she says she's an interior designer—she'd been acting goofy. Everything had to be perfect all the time. "I don't have the time to do everything anymore," she told us. "You kids have to help."

Everybody knows that when parents say "help," it really means you gotta do *everything*. It just wasn't fair. I never asked her to get a job.

Now I was forced to do all kinds of horrible things. Like cleaning up all the breakfast dishes, loading the dishwasher, and sweeping the floor. I didn't understand why Chuck couldn't help out at least a little.

I snarfed down the last of my Aunt Jemimas and

took a quick scan of the sports section. Chuck and my dad had already messed it up. I hate that. A guy deserves his paper all neat and crisp—not all floppy with butter and crumbs on it.

I read one headline: "Vikings Seem Ready for Packers." Yeah, right. Another said: "Twins to Be Aggressive in Free Agent Market." I laughed at that one. Everyone knew the Twins weren't going to sign anyone decent. Minnesota sports teams had really been in the dumper.

I started to clean up. As usual, Shea had already brought most of the dishes to the sink, pretty much doing my work for me. But the most important task was still ahead—the critical job of strategically placing the dishes in the dishwasher. Chuck might have been the star athlete of the family, but no one loaded a dishwasher like me. In fact, *Consumer Reports* once said I set the standard for maximizing upper-rack space.

I guess it's a gift.

Now, most people believe that dishes should be thoroughly rinsed before you stick them in the dishwasher, but c'mon—where's the sport in that? Modern dishwashers are high-performance machines. They don't need to be babied. The deal is, any lame dishwasher can clean a plate that's already been totally rinsed. But a real dishwasher demands the challenge of blasting off dried egg yolk. So I say let them fight the battles they were designed to fight. Let them be—dish*washers*.

And by skipping that whole dish-rinsing thing, you save about ten minutes.

By the time I finally finished in the kitchen, brushed my teeth, and got out the door, I was running about five minutes behind. I knew I could make it up by cutting through the park and around Keller Lake. I usually can't get away with this in November because of the snow. For some reason, though, we hadn't gotten any yet, so I still had an open path.

Even without the snow, it was crystal clear that winter had arrived. The icy wind blowing off Keller Lake dug deep into my cheeks like tiny little steak knives. My nose was running and my ears were cold, but somehow it all felt good.

It is my policy to never wear a hat before December. I also will not wear gloves before Christmas. After all, Minnesota is not for wimps (unless, of course, you play for the Vikings). You need to be tough to live in Minnesota. You can't be a crybaby when the snot freezes to your top lip and your earlobes get hard like Popsicles.

Another thing about us Minnesotans, we can spot an outsider from a billion miles away. I'm talking about the guys who just moved here from California or Des Moines or some other place. Those are the guys who start wearing parkas in September. And the geeks who wear snow boots before it snows. Those guys have no chance. They may as well just go jump off a cliff somewhere because they just aren't *ever* gonna make it here.

I rounded the western tip of the lake and headed for Sam's house. I live just one block outside the bus line. One block over, and I could've been riding a warm bus. Instead, I have to walk to school.

Chuck says this is stupid. He says I should just walk to the closest bus stop because it's still closer than walking all the way to school. But I am a guy with strong convictions. If they don't want me on their stinking bus, then I'll proudly walk.

Mitchie Evers may be a lot of things, but he is not a wimp.

2

DESPITE MY CALCULATIONS, I was still running behind schedule. I arrived at Sam's just about the time he was experiencing a massive coronary.

I guess Sam Travis is my very best friend, even though he drives me nuts. He's just so tense all the time.

"Finally, Mitchie," he barked as he burst out the door, his face red and his arms flapping. "We're gonna be late again. I don't need another tardy. I'm not gonna wait for you again if you're late."

"There you go again, Sam," I said, grabbing his backpack from him so he could finish putting on his jacket. "You're overreacting. We've got plenty of time. Big deal, so we miss first hour—"

"Miss first hour?" he screamed. "Are you nuts? Mitchie, you're gonna kill me."

"Sammy, I'm kidding. I'll have you there in plenty of time for first hour. Trust me."

"Did you get that paper done for Wapple?" he asked.

"I'm afraid Wapple will just have to wait," I replied. "I've been a little busy."

"Busy? You are so incredibly thick sometimes, Mitchie! You've known about it for a month. Wapple is not going to wait."

"You worry too much, Sam. In fact, you're starting to sound like my brother."

"Well, maybe you should listen to your brother."

"Now you're sounding like my mother."

"Maybe you should listen to her, too."

We sped it up the last couple of blocks and ran in the door of Keller Lake North Middle School with about three minutes to spare.

Sam sprinted to the other end of the school, where the eighth-grade lockers were.

I, on the other hand, strolled over to my locker, which was right next to the main entrance. These were the sixth-grade lockers, but I had traded with one of those little goofballs when school started so I wouldn't have to run around like Sam. I'd made the kid think he was getting the better end of the deal. Sixth-graders really don't get it.

I walked into Mr. Harris' science class just as the bell rang and sat at my table.

"Cutting it close once again, are we, Mr. Evers?" Harris asked as I plunked my backpack on the floor.

"Oh, you just got here too?" I replied.

I got a small laugh from the crowd.

"Mr. Evers, I'm curious where you developed your comedic skills," he said, walking slowly around his desk and pulling at his gray mustache. "It doesn't appear to be a family trait. Your brother didn't share your unique sense of humor when he was in my class. Maybe that's why he was such an outstanding student."

Trying to appear deadly serious, I looked down at my shoes and spoke quietly. "Well, we all wish Chuck had a better sense of humor, Mr. Harris. Maybe if he did, he wouldn't be fighting that terrible problem now." I looked up and paused before raising my voice. "Maybe if he had loosened up a bit, you know, had some fun once in a while, he wouldn't have snapped like that and—and . . . and now he wouldn't be locked up in that awful, awful place!"

I finished by pounding my fist on the desk and rubbing my eyes.

The class was silent. Harris looked at me funny. He struggled for a second or two, his left eye twitching— trying to figure out if I was for real. He didn't believe me, but at the same time he didn't want to take any chances.

"What exactly do you mean, Mr. Evers?" he asked.

"Oh, nothing, Mr. Harris," I said, straightening up and calmly taking my notebook and a pencil from my backpack. "I really shouldn't have said anything."

He kept his eyes on me as he walked slowly back to his podium. "Okay, eighth-graders," he started, still staring at me. "Let's review where we left off yesterday."

I swung around just long enough to get a look of disapproval from Annie, three chairs back and two rows over. Maybe disapproval was the wrong word. It was more like disbelief. Kind of like "You stupid jerk, why do you tell those stupid stories when you know nobody believes you?"

Annie Miles has lived across the street and one house down from me since we were both three. She has a sister the same age as Chuck, so she knew my brother wasn't locked away anywhere. But from the look in her blue eyes, I could tell she thought *I* should be.

At one time Annie and me were tight. When we were five, we'd pack lunches and take them to the park. Then we'd sit on top of the old metal slide and make believe we were astronauts shooting into outer space in a rocket. When we were six and seven, we'd ride our bikes along the forest path on the other side of Keller Lake and pretend we were on a secret journey deep into the rain forest. When we were eight, we'd send each other flashlight signals from our bedrooms.

By the time we were nine, it was not cool to hang around with a girl. So I did the next best thing.

I tormented her.

When Annie had friends over, me and Sam and the other guys would attack them with water balloons. When they camped out in Annie's backyard, we'd pull the stakes on the tent and wrap them up like fajitas. When she was dressed up nice, I'd go out of my way to tell her how geeky she looked.

It was just guy stuff, but Annie never thought it was funny. I don't know why. I think maybe it was because she had a big crush on me.

Anyway, when the bell finally rang again, waking

me from a light sleep, Annie stood in the classroom doorway, waiting for me.

"You really are a moron, aren't you?" she asked.

"I don't know," I said, getting up from my desk. "We're still waiting for the tests to come back."

She shook her head.

"What is it that Shea always tells you . . . you know, about your, uh, sense of humor?" she asked.

"She says I'm not funny," I answered.

"Well, she's right, Mitchell. It's time to find a new act."

I stopped and looked her in the eye. "Okay," I said. "But Shea is just a baby and can't possibly comprehend my humor. I think it all pretty much goes over your head too."

"Yeah, right, Mitchell," Annie said. "I don't think 'over my head' is exactly right. Most of your so-called jokes just lie there flat like *your* head." With that, she turned and stalked away.

Mitchell. Only two people in the world call me Mitchell—my mom and Annie.

Sam was waiting for me outside Wapple's English class. It was the only class we had together.

Sam's really a good guy, but like I said, he worries about everything. He worries about school. He worries when he sees lightning. He worries if his mom or dad is five minutes late. He worries when the cable on his TV goes out. He worries that someday he'll forget to change the clocks back when daylight savings time is over. And today he was worried because I hadn't finished the first draft of my paper for Wapple.

"I think you're in for it this time, Mitchie," he said as we walked in. "She looks serious today."

"Yeah, she looks serious," I said. "But not as serious as you. Geez, I remember when you used to be fun."

"And I remember when you weren't such a bonehead," Sam shot back as he took a desk in the back of the room.

I went up to old Ms. Wapple's desk and stood there, hoping she wouldn't notice me.

"What is it this time, Mitch?" she asked. "Aliens steal your homework?"

"No, Ms. Wapple," I said, doing my best to be humble. "It's just that I'm not as far along with my paper as I'd like to be."

"Not as far along as you'd like to be?" she asked. "What exactly does that mean?"

"Well, I'm not quite done with my—"

"All right, Mitch, stop right there. You didn't do it, did you?"

"I'm not quite—"

She didn't let me finish.

"Listen, the first time you pulled this, I gave you a break. Not this time. I think I made it clear how important this first draft is." Ms. Wapple dropped her pen to her desk and ran her hand across her forehead, pushing her silver bangs off to the side.

"This is how it's going to work," she said. "You bring me that first draft tomorrow, and I'll only drop your paper two full grades. You don't bring it tomorrow, you get an F on the whole thing. Got it?"

"But, Ms. Wapple—"

"End of discussion. Go sit down. I am really disappointed."

But before I could escape to my desk, she called me back.

"Mitch. You know what's so stupid about this?"

"No," I said, "but I'm sure you'll tell me."

"What's so stupid about this is that this would be pretty easy for you if you tried, even a little bit. You're really a strong writer—when you choose to be. Now, you're holding up this class, and I'm not going to allow that anymore."

I slunk back to my desk. Even Ms. Wapple was becoming immune to my charms.

I turned and looked at Sam. Our eyes met for an instant before he shook his head slowly and looked down at the notebook on his desk.

3

IT'S A LONG HAUL from Wapple's class to the gym, so I had to run the whole way. By the time I got to the locker room, everybody else was already in their gym clothes. I changed real fast and sped into the gym just in time to hear Coach Leonard blow his whistle.

Everybody stopped talking. No one messes with Coach Leonard. He's the football and wrestling coach. He used to be the head coach of the varsity football team over at the high school. They say he got sent down here because he was busted for beating his players. That's why no one messes with him.

"Okay, ladies," he said as we lined up on the mat. "Today we start our wrestling unit. But first, a couple of notes. Don't leave your wet towels on the floor by your lockers. Got it? I find one more wet towel on the floor, and I'm gonna crawl all over someone. And another thing—I want to talk to you boys about good hygiene . . ."

Sometimes I zone out when Coach Leonard starts lecturing. That's what must've happened, because the next thing I heard was:

"Evers, you know anything about this? *Evers!*"

"What, Coach?"

"Am I boring you?" Coach Leonard boomed. His skinny little arms, which poked out of his shirt like Q-Tips, were placed firmly on his hips. As mean and tough as he is, Coach Leonard is one skinny little guy. However, that doesn't make him look any less scary.

"No, you're not boring me at all, Coach," I said. "You know I've always found you both entertaining and informative."

"Well," he said, thinking about that for a second, "do you know anything about my bulletin boards being messed up?"

"No," I said, and I was telling the truth. Only an idiot would mess with Coach Leonard's bulletin boards. "I don't know who would do such a thing. You know how much we all enjoy your bulletin boards."

This time I might have laid it on too thick.

"You know how much we all enjoy your bulletin boards," he shot back, mimicking me. "Are you being wise, Evers?"

"Not at all, Coach," I said.

"Good," he said. "Because I hate wise guys. Okay, let's wrestle. And, Evers, since we've already enjoyed such a nice conversation, why don't you and I demonstrate for the class, huh?"

Now I *knew* I'd gone too far. Demonstrating for the class was Coach Leonard's way of sticking it to you. I'd seen this happen before. And it wasn't pretty.

"Come on, Evers, don't be shy," he said. "I *love* to wrestle, and I'm sure you do too."

I walked slowly to the center of the mat.

"Let's start with takedowns," he said. "On the whistle."

He didn't wait one second. He blew the whistle, lunged for me, grabbed me by the legs, and flipped me up in the air and then flat onto my back on the mat. He squeezed me like he was folding me into an envelope, held me like that for a few seconds, then rolled off and slapped the mat.

"Fall!" he barked. I just lay there twisted and in pain. The coach had made his point.

"See that, wrestlers? A two-legged takedown followed by a half nelson inside crotch for the pin. Any questions? That's what we're gonna work on. Now pair up with someone your size. Cristobal, you come here and work with Evers. He should be easy. I've already softened him up for you."

I slowly got to my feet, only to see the fire in Cristobal's eyes. Cristobal's not a bad guy, but he's like one of those gentle giants who doesn't know how strong he is. I spent the next thirty minutes being flipped around like a dog's chew toy.

The gym is far from the lunchroom, so as soon as the bell rang, I had to jump in the shower, get dressed, and fly to get my lunch and find the guys. I caught up with Sammy in the lunch line. Sammy's one of those guys who actually eats the school food.

I reminded him about Chuck's game. "Tonight," I said. "Be ready at six-thirty."

He rolled his eyes. "Six-thirty?" he asked. "Why so early?"

"Because it's the last game, and my mom doesn't want to miss anything."

"But geez, Mitchie, it's gonna be freezing," he whined, "and we're gonna be there forever."

"Oh, quit being a baby," I said. "Just wear lots of clothes."

"You going to the game tonight?" asked the Weasel as we sat down at our usual table. We call him the Weasel because he looks like one. He's a good guy, but he really does have a face like a rodent. He also has a habit of asking the world's most obvious questions.

"Well, I don't know," I said. "Let's see. I've been to every Keller Lake High varsity soccer game for the last three years. Tonight is the last home game of the season. And my brother, who's only a junior, is probably gonna set the new all-time school scoring record. Naw, Weasel, I'll probably just stay home tonight and play Barbies with my little sister."

He looked at me funny.

There are usually about eight of us who eat lunch together. There's me and Sam, John Falcone, Lance Higginbothom (the Weasel), Mark "Kozmo" Kozmorowski, Sid Bestler, Steve Schack, and Brooks Maggert, who we all call Maggot, which drives him nuts. They're all good guys, even though Maggot and the Weasel can be pretty nerdy at times.

Most of us have played on the same soccer team for about a hundred years. All except for Sammy and Maggot. Sid quit playing last year, but he was never very good anyway. The rest of us all played together on this year's eighth-grade team. That is, we played together for most of the season.

"So is Chuck gonna do it, or what?" asked Falcone from across the table.

"Do what?" I asked, even though I knew just what he meant.

"Break the record, dopeface," he said, shoving an entire half of a peanut butter sandwich into his mouth, the crumbs falling all over his red sweatshirt.

"Does it really matter?" I asked. "I mean, is it really about records? Isn't it about playing for the love of the game?"

"You're full of crap, Mitchie," Falcone said in as nice a way as possible.

"Hey, Mitchie," said the Weasel from the other end of the group. "The real question is, are you and Hendricks gonna go at it again today? You better be careful. I think he's gonna blow up pretty soon."

"Let him blow," I said. Hendricks was my math teacher. He used to be my soccer coach. "I'd love to see little pieces of his precious warm-up suit come floating down like confetti."

I didn't think what I'd said was all that funny, but the Weasel is an easy audience. He laughed so hard, he snorted milk out his nose.

I always enjoy that, so pretty soon I was laughing too.

AFTER LUNCH, I MADE MY way to math. The Weasel was right. Things had been heating up between me and Hendricks.

Basically, he was doing everything he could to make me miserable. I'm pretty good in math, but it seemed like he'd call on me only for the really hard problems, just to show me up. And he always had a comment on what I was wearing or how I was sitting in my seat or how stuffed my backpack was.

And, of course, I couldn't just let stuff like that go. I always had to say something. And even though I knew I should just lie low and stay out of his way, I found myself doing everything I could to annoy him.

The fact is, every second in his classroom just reminded me of how badly he'd messed everything up for me.

He started class the same way he always did, by trying to make some lame joke. Nobody laughed.

After a few minutes, he was into his regular routine. He was drawing a problem on the board, and he got so into it, he started swinging his arms around in huge sweeping gestures. I couldn't tell if he thought he was an orchestra conductor or one of those guys with the red flashlights who directs the airplanes into the terminal.

His back was to the class, so I stood up. I know it was stupid. But I just couldn't stop myself.

There I was, standing behind Hendricks, copying his movements and throwing my arms around like a windmill. The Weasel was doing everything he could to keep from laughing out loud. The rest of the class started to twitch, and Hendricks must have sensed that.

He turned from the board quickly. I plopped back

to my seat and started rubbing my arm real hard, like I was having a spasm.

Hendricks just stood there for a second, knowing something was going on but not sure exactly what. He also knew I was in the middle of it.

"Evers," he said. "Is everything all right?"

"Sure," I said. "I just got a cramp. It's fine now."

He started walking toward me. He looked mad.

"I don't know what you were doing," he said with fire in his eyes. "But don't do it again. Don't distract this class. Understood?"

"Understood," I said. I did understand, but I really didn't care. I just couldn't think of anything he could do to me that was worse than what he'd already done.

The instant class was over, me and my backpack were out the door.

4

WE PICKED UP SAMMY late for Chuck's game that night, which was normal.

There wasn't much of a crowd. It was cold, and Chuck's team had no chance of making the playoffs, even if they won tonight.

The only thing that made this game important was the possibility of Chuck's breaking the scoring record. If Chuck scored two goals, he'd become the all-time leading scorer in Keller Lake Skippers history. And since he was only a junior, he had another whole year to play.

My mom and dad and Shea sat with the rest of the parents, and me and Sammy snuck down on the field like we always did. You're not supposed to be able to do that, but when your brother's the star of the team and you don't get in the way, nobody really cares.

The first quarter was boring. The other team—the Lakeville Panthers—was in last place. The Skippers should've been pounding them, but Chuck's coach was playing all the second- and third-string guys who hadn't played much during the season. Chuck only played a minute or two in the first quarter.

Everybody knew Chuck was going for the record,

even the Lakeville guys. And when Chuck came out to start the second quarter, you could tell they weren't gonna let him anywhere near the goal. I was trying very hard to act like I wasn't paying attention, like I really didn't care. But something happens to me when I get near a field or a rink. It's almost eerie. I see everything. It's like everything slows down for me and I can see every move on the field. My coaches have always called me a smart player. I don't know if I'm all that smart, but I always seem to know where the ball or the puck is gonna go before it gets there. I know that sounds kind of like I'm bragging. But I'm not. I just see plays develop.

And I could really see how the Lakeville jerks were just beating the heck out of Chuck. I mean, he couldn't turn left without three guys pounding him. Once, this little guy slid at Chuck and knocked his feet right out from under him. And Chuck didn't even have the ball. It was one of the dirtiest plays I'd ever seen. The guy could've blown out Chuck's knee.

I, of course, would've ripped the guy's head off. But not Chuck. After Chuck got up, he held out his hand to the jerk and helped *him* up.

When Chuck came out for the second half, he looked even more wired than normal. He definitely had something on his mind, and I knew he was gonna score in a hurry.

And he did. He took a pass from midfield, faked out one of the defenders, and had a clear and open shot at the goal. But he didn't take it.

Instead, Chuck held on to the ball, dribbled toward

the guy who'd made that dirty play in the first half, and then he just sort of stopped. The Lakeville guy didn't know what to do. After about a second, he tried to take the ball, but Chuck pulled it back like he had it on a string. The Lakeville player almost did the splits, trying to go in two directions at the same time. He tried to recover, but Chuck beat him like a drum, dancing in and firing a shot into the low left corner for a goal.

As Chuck ran back to midfield, he stopped and—once again—helped the dirty, scummy Lakeville player up. Only this time he stared right into the guy's skull, burning lasers into the guy's eye sockets. And then Chuck smiled this sinister smile. It said all there was to say. It said, "Go ahead, you cheap jerk. Play dirty. I'll just twist you like a pretzel and score whenever I feel like it." This Lakeville guy had to be popping some serious goose bumps. I don't think he went anywhere near Chuck the rest of the game.

I looked up in the stands after that first goal and saw my mom jumping up and down like a crazy person. My dad was high-fiving the guy in front of him.

I couldn't remember their doing that when I scored. But then, it had been so long since I'd even been on the field . . .

The announcer's voice boomed through the stadium: *"With that goal, junior forward Chuck Evers has tied the all-time goal-scoring record for the Keller Lake Skippers."* My mom jumped up again, and there was a lot of clapping. Sammy started to yell.

"Relax, Sammy," I said.

"Your brother just tied the record. You can't even get a little excited?"

"There's enough people up there clapping for him," I said. "He can't hear me anyway."

It *was* an incredible play, and I don't know why I wasn't juiced. Maybe it was because I was really starting to realize that I was probably never, ever gonna play on this field.

And that just seemed wrong.

See, this wasn't just Chuck's field. It was mine too. He wasn't gonna be the only record setter here. I was supposed to come up next year. Then I'd own this place just like he did.

But that was before.

I looked out from the sideline and took it all in. The players, the lights, the crowd, the fresh white lines on the field, the press box, and the cheerleaders.

I was gonna be right out there, right smack-dab in the middle of it.

I was gonna own this place.

Yeah, right.

I heard the crowd go nuts again, and Sammy started jumping up and down.

"He did it again! Geez, he's incredible, Mitchie. Did you see that goal?"

"No," I lied. "Was it nice?"

"Nice?" he said. "It was the prettiest goal I've ever seen. What were you doing?"

I might have been *thinking* about something else, but the truth is, I saw the play. I saw every move. Like I said—on a soccer field I see everything. And

Sam was right. It was an even better goal than the first one. Sam hadn't even noticed Chuck's no-look pass one second before that set up the whole play. But I did.

"Chuck Evers is now the all-time leading goal scorer in Keller Lake Skippers history!" roared the announcer.

I watched as all the guys on the field came over and gave him high fives and stuff. But he wasn't smiling. Knowing Chuck, I'm sure he was thinking, "We still have a game to play. There'll be time for celebrating later."

Man, are we different. If that was me, I'd have been bouncing off the goalposts. I'd have been running up and down the field waving at the crowd, ripping off my jersey and throwing it to my fans.

Geez, I would've been *drowning* in it. And there was my lame brother setting this huge record and acting like it was no big deal.

And then I thought again, "Man, if that was me . . ."

But then I remembered. It wasn't me.

It was never gonna be me.

AFTER THE GAME, CHUCK went out with the guys on his team. I just went up to my room. I had no interest in doing Wapple's stupid paper, even though she was right. I could do it in my sleep.

Instead, I just lay on my bed and bounced a tennis ball off the wall. Then my dad walked in.

"Big night, huh?" he asked, standing at the foot of my bed.

"Yeah, Chuck was great," I said, staring at the ceiling.

He stood there for a second. Then he asked, "Is something going on with you two?"

"No, nothing's going on," I replied. "Nothing at all. In fact, I don't think he's talked to me for about a month."

"Well," Dad said, "you haven't been a lot of fun to talk to lately."

I sat up and turned to face him. "Dad, you just don't get it," I said.

"That's right," he snapped. "I don't." He shook his head, turned, and left.

I rolled back and resumed my ball tossing.

I did that for a few more minutes; then I heard Chuck walk into his room. For a second I thought about going in and saying something, maybe something about how cool it was that he broke the record.

But instead I got up, grabbed my backpack, and sat at my desk to write that stupid rough draft for Wapple.

Somehow, it just seemed easier than talking to Chuck.

5

WHEN I WALKED INTO the kitchen for breakfast the next morning, I was quickly reminded that Chuck was going to finally and officially introduce his girlfriend to the Evers family that night at dinner.

It had somehow slipped my mind.

We'd been hearing about "Susan" for what seemed like forever, but nobody in the family had actually met her.

And now she was coming to our house for dinner. I wondered if anybody had alerted the news media.

I ate my breakfast in a hurry, loaded the dishwasher, and scrambled out the door. When I got to Sam's, he was still talking about Chuck.

"I keep thinking about that second goal, Mitchie," he said, his glasses bouncing up and down on his nose with every step. "I've never seen anybody else do that. Ever!"

"Geez, Sammy. I taught him that move."

"Yeah, right," he said. "Hey, what did he say about it? Was he jumping around the house or was he just acting like normal old Chuck?"

"I don't know," I said. "I haven't even seen him."

"What do you mean you haven't seen him? It's your brother's biggest night ever, and you haven't even talked to—"

"Oh, relax, Sammy," I said. "I was working on that paper for Wapple. Remember, the one you were bugging me about all day yesterday?"

"Yeah," he said with a funny look in his eyes. "But you'd think you'd at least stop by his room, say 'Hey, way to become like the greatest soccer star in Keller Lake history.'"

"Yeah," I said. "You'd think so."

I couldn't sit still all day. Just thinking about Hendricks and Chuck and everything else was making me twitch. So at lunch, I made plans with the guys for a touch football game after school. A touch football game always made me feel better.

Plus, I needed to blow off some steam.

By the time I walked into Hendricks' class, I was in some kind of mental vapor lock. I wasn't even thinking when Laura Wannamaker handed me the note from the Weasel. I took my time reading the mangled hunk of paper. The Weasel never got any points for neatness. And the note was so stupid. The Weasel was asking where we were gonna play our game. "Geez, I don't know," I thought, "maybe *we'll play in the exact same place* we've played *every other* touch football game we've *ever played!*"

Suddenly, I felt the coach's hot breath on my neck.

"Are we interrupting your reading, Evers?"

"This?" I asked, leaning back and crossing my legs. "Just some fan mail. You know how it is. Or then again, you probably don't. I mean, you'd actually have to have some fans—"

And that's when the Weasel's prediction came true.

Hendricks blew.

"All right, that's it!" he bellowed, his face turning purple. "I've had it with you, Evers!"

"Well, that's fine!" I said, jumping to my feet. "I've had it with you, too!"

We stood there for a second, neither of us saying anything. The room was silent.

I could tell he was trying to cool down.

"Go out in the hall and wait for me," he said finally.

The room stayed silent. Hendricks turned and walked to the front of the room. I calmly threw my notebook in my backpack, hoisted the pack onto my left shoulder, and walked out the door.

When I got outside, I pulled off my backpack, dropped it, and with my back against the wall, slid down until I was sitting on the floor.

My head was pounding. This was not good.

I heard him before I saw him.

He slammed the door shut behind him and grabbed me by my elbow.

"Okay, Evers," he said. "Let's get down to business."

"Don't blame all this on me," I said. "You've been on my back since the first day of school."

"You think so, huh?" He was two inches from my face. "I've been a little rough, have I? Well, maybe that's because I thought you could take it. Maybe I thought you were tough, like your brother."

"Will you stop it with the all the brother stuff?" I yelled. "I'm sorry I didn't score as many goals as he did. I'm sorry I wasn't the team leader like he was. I'm sorry his hair is brown and mine is blond. But most of all, I'm just sorry I'm stuck with you for math."

"Well, we can fix that," said Hendricks.

Then it was quiet for a minute.

"You don't get it, do you?" Hendricks finally asked. "God, you frustrate me, Evers."

"Well, I guess it doesn't really matter now, does it?" I said. "Because I'm not even playing anymore."

"That was your choice, hotshot!"

Hendricks rubbed his forehead, then started talking again. "Look, no one ever expected you to be your brother. I didn't move you to forward because your brother was a forward. I moved you there because you were the team's best shooter and we needed some scoring. I didn't expect you to be a team leader because your brother was. I expected you to be a team leader because, like it or not, it's usually the better players who become the leaders. And you should have been our best player."

He was on a roll.

"And finally," Hendricks said. "I don't expect you to be a good math student because your brother was. I didn't even have your brother in math. I expect you to be a good math student because you're capable of being a good math student."

He finally stopped to take a breath. I could see he was mad, but he also looked kind of confused, like he just couldn't figure me out. Then he started again.

"That's the point, wise guy. You're not doing anything as well as you can. Nothing. And it's just a waste. Could you be as good a soccer player as your brother? Probably not. He was the best I ever coached. But you have all the tools to be an excellent player, maybe even *one* of the best. But you don't care. This whole brother obsession of yours is just another way for you to take the easy way out. Well, go ahead. But you're not going to disrupt my class ever again. Now, go down and see Mr. Pendleton. And don't come back to this class until you're ready to learn something."

I couldn't think of anything to say, so I shot him a look.

But Hendricks just stood there and slowly shook his head.

6

WALKED INTO THE principal's office. Mrs. Jenkins was there to greet me.

She was incredibly scary. It was like somebody had painted her eyebrows on with a huge marker. Her hair was stacked up on top of her head and it looked like it would just crumble to dust if you touched it. The giant mole on her left cheek looked like some kind of serious skin fungus.

"Coach Hendricks already called down, so Mr. Pendleton is expecting you," Mrs. Jenkins said without looking up. "Have a seat. He'll be with you in a minute."

"What's he doing?" I asked. "Forcing a confession from some kid?"

In her eighty-four years as a principal's secretary, Mrs. Jenkins had heard it all. I wasn't surprised when she didn't even flinch. "I said he'll be with you in a minute."

When Pendleton came out, I was leafing through a two-year-old copy of *Highlights*. He didn't look happy. "Come on in," he said, a large manila folder in his hand.

I sat down in the plastic-and-metal chair across from his desk. On the shelf behind him were pictures of his family.

"You have a beautiful family, Mr. Pendleton," I said.

"Knock off the crap," he shot back. "I'm not in the mood."

I looked out the window. I should have known better than to try and work Pendleton. He'd been my baseball coach in seventh grade, and he knew me pretty well.

He didn't say anything for a moment or two, just leafed through the file.

Then, without looking up, he asked, "What's with you, Mitchie? What's the deal here?"

I didn't answer.

He leaned back in his chair and flopped one of his huge feet over an open file drawer. I saw the bare trees behind him bending hard in the wind.

"You said some things to Coach Hendricks today you shouldn't have, huh, Mitchie?" he asked.

"Yeah, I guess it's my trademark."

"Well, it must be, because I've heard from both Wapple and Harris this week, and now Hendricks. And let's face it, your grades aren't what they could be—not anywhere close. Last year you were the model student. This year I feel like I'm watching a guy doing everything he can to put himself in a jam."

"Look," I said. "I missed a deadline with Wapple. Harris has no sense of humor. And my problems with

Hendricks have to do with soccer, not math. We're not talking about a life of crime here, so don't worry about anything."

Pendleton shifted forward in his chair and looked into my eyes.

"What is the story with you and Coach Hendricks?" he asked. "I know it's harder sometimes when your coach is also your teacher. But this is getting out of control."

"It's nothing I can't handle," I said.

"Right, Mitchie," Pendleton said. "That's why you're here and not in math. Look, you need to work this out. I think you're right, your problems with the coach started with soccer. What really happened? I never heard the whole story."

He was talking about the "incident."

"It was a long time ago," I said. "It really doesn't matter."

"It was three weeks ago," he answered. "And of course it matters."

I thought for a second. It was complicated. I really didn't want to get into it.

"Look," I offered, "we just didn't agree on how I should play the game."

"That's why he kicked you off the team?"

I jumped to my feet. "He didn't kick me off. I quit."

"So it's okay to be a quitter?" he asked.

"That's not what I mean. It's just that everyone thinks I got kicked off and that's not what happened."

"Then tell me what happened."

"You sure you want to hear all this?"

"I've got nowhere to go—and neither do you."

I paused for a few seconds.

"Okay," I said. "Me and Falcone were singing on the bus after we lost to Cannon Falls, and Coach basically went nuts. He started yelling that we had nothing to be happy about. By then, I'd had enough of his abuse. I'd been taking it all year. So I just told him to lay off, that we'd played the best we could."

"And he didn't like that?" asked Pendleton.

"Not at all," I answered. "He said that wouldn't have been good enough for my brother. And that's when *I* blew. I'd been hearing that all year too. So I told him Chuck wasn't on our team, and that he— Coach Hendricks—was stuck with me."

I stopped for a second, looked down at my shoes, then started again.

"Right there he demoted me to the third line. I told him to forget it; if he didn't want me around, I'd just quit. He said that was fine too. So I quit."

"In other words," Pendleton said after a few moments, "you went from being a starter to the third line to being an ex–soccer player in about fifteen seconds?"

"That's about it."

He thought about that for a second.

"Well, why do you think the coach was leaning on you so much?" he said.

"That's easy," I said. "From the very beginning Hendricks thought I was going to be a clone of my brother. He wanted me to play like him, act like him—just be like him. And I'm not like him at all."

"That's quite a story, Mitchie," Pendleton said. "Any regrets?"

"Sure," I said. "I regret that he was my coach—and my math teacher."

Pendleton leaned back in his chair again. "You know what I mean."

"Yeah," I said. "I wish I was still playing. But it doesn't matter. When he took me out of the midfield, he ruined my chances of making varsity next year, so what's the point?"

"Why was playing varsity next year so important?" asked Pendleton.

"Forget it," I said. "You wanted to know what happened with me and Hendricks. And now you know. What's next?"

"I have to call your parents."

"Great," I said. "Call my parents. Geez, I have one small 'discussion' with my math teacher and suddenly I'm like two steps from reform school."

"Mitchie," Pendleton said, sliding the file drawer shut. "There are procedures for getting you back in class, and one of those is notifying your parents. You're also looking at after-school detention, probably three days—"

"Three days?" I yelped. "Forget it. I didn't *do* anything. Hendricks started it."

"See, Mitchie, that's something that worries me," he said. "It's always someone else's fault with you." He paused. "Look, I can't fix your soccer problem, but I can help you with your math situation. However, you need to start using your head."

He looked up at the clock behind me. "Okay, the bell's about to ring. Get to your next class, and keep your head down the rest of the day. I don't want to have to call in the police."

"Very funny," I thought. He could afford to be a comedian. *He* wasn't looking at after-school detention. Nobody would be calling *his* parents.

"When are you gonna call my mom?" I asked him.

"You're lucky," he said. "I have to race out of here right now to get to my daughter's doctor's appointment. I'll call your parents tomorrow. That also gives you a reprieve from detention today."

I left Pendleton's office feeling like I wanted to pound somebody. And looking back, that probably wasn't the best frame of mind for me to have going into a friendly game of touch football.

7

THE TRUTH IS, THERE are few things better than playing touch football in the fall in Minnesota, and I tried to keep my mind on that as I made my way to the field.

Starting when I was about three, me and Chuck would go out in the front yard and replay that Sunday's entire Vikings game. We'd take turns being each team. One play, I'd be the Vikings' running back taking the ball in for the go-ahead touchdown. The next play, Chuck would be the big defensive lineman, sacking me in the end zone for a safety.

When I got a little bigger, my dad would be the quarterback, and Chuck and I would alternate between being the pass receiver and the pass defender. Chuck had the advantage, of course, because he was bigger and stronger, but my dad would always throw the ball in a spot where we could both reach it. Then we'd battle it out. Chuck always caught more passes than I did, but I never gave up. I'd scrap all the way, fighting for every pass. I think my dad liked that.

Shea would run around and chase us, always about

ten steps behind the play. She always cheered for me. She'd yell, "Mitchie, Mitchie, don't let Chuck get it!" and "Watch out, watch out, Chuck's gonna get the football! Stop him, Mitchie!"

Even then she was a bright kid.

When she turned six, she started doing the play-by-play, copying what she heard on TV: "Dad takes the snap and drops back to pass. Mitchie runs down the field, covered by Chuck. Mitchie catches the pass. He—could—go—*all—the—way*!"

One time, we ran a little swing pattern over by the south side of the house, right where Shea was jumping around. My dad threw a bullet chest-high that both Chuck and I reached for, but it was cold and he threw it too hard. The football bounced off my frozen fingers and smacked right into Shea's face.

By the time we got to her, blood was gushing from both nostrils. Even though the tears were running and her face was beet red, she wasn't crying out loud. She just looked up and said, "I'm okay, Mitchie, but next time catch the stupid ball." Then her eyes lit up. "Do you think maybe next time I should wear a football helmet?"

Later that day, I borrowed some money from Chuck and rode my bike down to Walgreens and bought Shea one of those costume football helmets. You know, those cheap plastic ones that say on the inside THIS IS NOT A PROTECTIVE DEVICE AND SHOULD NOT BE WORN IN COMPETITIVE ACTION. She thought it was the coolest thing in the world and she didn't take it off for two days. She even tried to eat with it on, and she got the face mask covered with applesauce. I still have the picture of her with her helmet on. It's in my room over my desk.

I think it might be my favorite picture of Shea.

I still play a lot of touch football, but not with my family. Once in a while I toss it around with Shea, but Chuck is just way too busy being a soccer star. I think me and my dad tossed the football around once last year. But this fall, forget it. He's been tied up with school.

I WAS THE LAST GUY to get to the park. We have the perfect place to play football at Keller Lake Park. On one side is the Parkers' yard, which has two pine trees about fifty yards apart that work as perfect goal line markers.

The other end zone is the beach, so you can dive into the sand for low passes and not get hurt (at least until it freezes). Once, Sammy dived too close to the shore and got a little wet. Since it was only about forty-five degrees, we had to get him home before he froze to death. But he made a truly great catch, probably his greatest of all time.

When I got to the field, the other seven guys were already kicking and throwing the ball around. I like playing with these guys because they all play pretty hard. But after the day I'd had, I guess I should've warned them all to stay out of my way.

"Okay, you goofballs," I called. "What are the teams?"

Falcone said, "How about me, Sid, the Weasel, and Sam against you, Kozmo, Schack, and Maggot?"

"Hey!" Maggot yelled. "Quit calling me *Maggot*!"

"Fine," I said. "Those are the teams."

"Okay," said the Weasel, jumping up and down spastically. "Are we gonna stand around all day like a bunch of women, or are we gonna play some football?"

"We'll kick off," I called out as I ran back with my teammates.

Maggot took the ball from Sam, and they walked toward the line of pine trees on the right.

We play two-hand touch below the waist, razzle-dazzle on the kickoff. That means you gotta touch a guy with both hands below the waist to get him down. Razzle-dazzle on the kickoff means the team that gets the ball can pass the football to a teammate on the kickoff. It makes kickoffs pretty cool.

"Who wants to kick?" I asked.

"Anybody but you," said Schack, walking slowly upfield. "You can't kick."

"Bite me," I snapped back.

The wind off the lake was cool on my face as I waited for Schack to kick. Our rules say you gotta give the guy on the other team time to catch the kick before you can nail him. But I was pretty charged up as I ran down the field.

I didn't give Sid a second. I came at him full blast. I clapped his hips hard with both hands, almost before he could get control of the ball.

"You're down!" I yelled.

He threw the ball down. "Yeah, I'm down," he said. "Geez, am I supposed to get some time to catch the ball, or what?"

"I *gave* you time," I barked.

"Yeah, right," he said, walking back to huddle up with his teammates.

"Oh, Mitchie," whined the Weasel in his squeaky rodentlike voice. "A little wound up, are we?"

"Weasel," I said. "Why don't you come over here and kiss my big toe—the one with the fungus on it?"

"Knock it off," Sam said. "Let's play football."

I set out wide to cover the Weasel. Sid dropped back to pass, and I had the Weasel covered. But somehow, Sammy got loose. Suddenly he came out of nowhere and made the catch. By the time I could turn around, Sammy was already down the field and heading in for a touchdown.

"Geez, Maggot!" I yelled. "You off picking your nose somewhere, or what?"

Kozmo looked at me funny. "Relax, Mitchie," he said. "It's just a game. Maybe you need a vacation."

I was really steamed. My *grandma* could cover Sammy.

So now it was Sid kicking off to us.

"I'll take the kick," I said.

"Sure you will, you ball hog," snapped Kozmo.

I turned around and started walking toward him.

"I'm a ball hog, huh, Kozmo?" I asked, my face getting red.

"Whatever, Mitchie," he said. "You know you are. I've only called you that about a billion times."

He was right, but this time it really irritated me.

It was a weak kick, and it ended up going to Kozmo anyway. He ran for about five yards before they forced him out of bounds. It was our ball, first down.

Maggot, Schack, Kozmo, and I huddled together to map out our plan. Kozmo is fast, but he's got no hands. Maggot is slow, but he catches anything you throw to him. Schack's a pretty good athlete, but it's like his arms are too short. He can never reach the football when I throw it to him.

"Okay, look," I said. "Kozmo, you take the Weasel deep. Maggot, you cut across the middle and take Sid with you. Schack, stay in like you're looking to block, then curl off to your right. I'll hit you in the flat. Let's fool 'em a little bit."

Kozmo snapped the ball back to me and I dropped back to pass. But they were blitzing. All four guys came flying in, and I had no time to do anything. I tried to throw the ball over the Weasel's outstretched arms, but he batted it down, right into Sammy's hands. Sammy took the football, spun upfield, and headed toward the end zone with the interception.

I was not going to let Sam Travis beat me—again.

I turned myself around, found my footing, and started after him. He had a big lead, but I'm a lot faster, so I gained on him in a hurry. By the time he reached the pine tree, I was just about there. With one last rush, I dived and slapped both of my hands on his right hip. Maybe I gave him a little more of a smack than I needed to.

The contact knocked him flying, and he hit the

base of the pine tree, still holding on to the football. Sammy scored the touchdown, but he'd come down real hard on his left shoulder, and I could tell he was in pain.

He got up slowly. Then he started screaming at me.

"Geez, Mitchie! Are you trying to kill me? You're a maniac!" With that, he took the ball and launched a perfect spiral that nailed me square in my right thigh.

It may have been his greatest pass ever.

It stung bad, but I wasn't gonna let him know that.

"What was that for?" I asked. "I wasn't trying to cream you. You just slipped."

Sammy took a step toward me. "Slipped? You nearly killed me." With that, he stomped away, wiping pine needles off his clothes, readjusting the strap on his glasses, and wiping his nose with the sleeve of his flannel shirt.

"C'mon, Sammy," I said. "I didn't mean to knock you over."

"I'm done," he said, working his arm around in a big circle. "My shoulder hurts. I'm going home."

"Aw, Sammy," I said. "Don't be a baby."

"A baby," he said, his glasses nearly steaming over. "You come out here like a maniac, yelling at everybody, and then you start slamming guys around, and I'm a baby? I guess I'm just a little tired of being in the middle of your mental breakdown, Mitchie. You need therapy." Then he stomped off.

The other guys just kind of stood there. Sammy

didn't normally blow up like that. No one knew what to say.

"You must've really creamed his shoulder," said Maggot.

"Shut up, Maggot," I said.

"Quit calling me *Maggot*!"

"Here's a little secret," I yelled back as I walked away. "We call you Maggot because you smell like one."

The last thing I heard was Maggot in the background going, "Geez, what did I do?"

I took the long way home from the park.

I felt pretty bad. I knew I shouldn't have given Maggot that last shot. That one didn't even feel good.

It was getting colder and darker. Without snow, the park was really bleak. The grass was brown and the naked trees seemed to be looking down, laughing at me.

We really needed some snow.

I truly hadn't meant to hammer Sammy, but I sure as heck hadn't wanted him to score, either.

Sammy being mad at me was really nothing new. In fact, I think Sam was mad at me for the entire sixth grade. But even though I jerked him around a lot, there was just something about us that made us stay together—even though we always seemed to annoy the heck out of each other.

A year and a half ago, I got mono. I felt so crummy I thought I was gonna die. As soon as the doctors said it was okay, Sammy came over every day, bringing me comic books and playing video games with me. My mom still talks about it. I never thought it was such a big deal. I just thought he had nothing better to do.

There are a lot of guys I play football and hockey with, a lot of guys I hang with at school. But I really have only one truly close friend.

And I had just run him into a pine tree.

THINGS WEREN'T MUCH better when I got home. I walked right into the big Susan dinner, and it was all just too much for me to take.

I ditched out before dessert and hid up in my room. I didn't even say good-bye or good night to anyone.

I got into bed and pulled the covers up over my head.

I just wanted the day to end.

8

AT BREAKFAST THE NEXT morning, Shea could tell I was still in a bad mood.

"What's wrong, Mitchie?" she asked between bites of Froot Loops. "Lose your best friend?"

"What's that supposed to mean?" I snapped, slamming down the sports page.

"It's just an expression," she answered. "Like 'it's hotter than blazes' or something like that. You don't have to yell at me."

"Is my Mitchell yelling at my little girl?" asked Mom as she walked into the kitchen. "You better be careful, Mitchell. I think Shea can take you."

"You know it, Mom," Shea said.

"So what's going on here?" Mom asked. "You're moving pretty slowly this morning, Mitchell."

She was right. I wasn't even dressed yet.

"I better stay home today, Mom. I think I'm sick."

Shea walked over and felt my forehead. "Do you think it's a tumor, Mitchie? Maybe your appendix is going to explode. Or it could be scarlet fever."

"It's not scarlet fever," I grumbled. "I'm glad you find it so funny, you little twerp. I *am* sick. I really am."

"Well, you're not fooling me," my mom said. "Now, get upstairs and get ready for school. Shea and I have to leave." She turned to my sister, who was busily loading her book bag. "Go brush your teeth, Shea."

Then Mom stopped and turned toward me with a big smile on her face. "What about that Susan?" she asked. "Chuck's got quite a girl there, doesn't he?"

I was pouring milk over my Frosted Flakes and didn't look up.

"Well?" she asked again.

"What, Mom?" I said, still not looking up.

"I said, isn't Susan pretty sharp?"

"She's *wonderful*," I replied.

My mom looked annoyed. "Oh, come on, Mitchell, I can't remember the last time I heard you say anything nice about anybody." She and Shea turned and left.

Suddenly Shea came bouncing back in, her hat pulled down nearly to her chin.

"Don't forget, Mitchie, tonight's the night."

"For what?"

"You know, *Cool Planet* comes out tonight on video. Remember?" She tapped on my head with her knuckles. "We're gonna watch it? You know, like we've been talking about for about a million years? Remember?"

I shoved in another bite of Frosted Flakes and turned. "Oh, right," I said. "It's gonna be the highlight of my week."

Shea looked at me. "Okay," she said after a moment. "But don't forget."

Then I heard the door slam.

I'd never been much of a science fiction guy, but Shea ate that junk up. I took her to see *Cool Planet* when it opened at the theater last year, and she made me promise to rent it for her the minute it came out on video so she could see it again.

I really didn't want to see the dumb movie again, even though I *had* promised her.

I didn't hurry loading the dishwasher. I was pretty sure Sam wasn't gonna wait for me anyway. I brushed my teeth, threw on my old ripped-up plaid flannel shirt, a pair of jeans, and my beat-up brown boots— the ones my mom can't stand—and headed for the door.

Maybe it was because I was tired, but I headed down Keller Lane without paying any attention. That's why my early-warning system failed to pick up Annie, who was coming up on me from behind.

"Yo, Mitchell," she screamed from about two houses down.

Knowing I was about to be sucked into the Annie gravitational field, I decided to pretend I didn't hear her.

It didn't work.

"What are you, deaf?" she asked, running up alongside me.

I turned and looked at her. Then I took my hands out of my pockets and started doing sign language.

"No, Mitchell," she said. "You're stupid, not deaf."

"Oh, that's right," I said, not breaking stride. "I always get that wrong. I'm stupid, not deaf. And you, Annie, you're really ugly, right?"

"Actually, Mitchell," she said, "I'm considered quite cute. And I'm still pretty popular, too. You, on the other hand, have no friends left."

"Where do you get this stuff?" I asked. "I mean, was this on the network news or something? Or maybe somebody spray-painted it on the side of a building."

"Typical Mitchell Evers," Annie said. "You lose your best friend, and you're making jokes. I'm serious, Mitchell, you keep mouthing off and someone's gonna smack you."

"First of all, Sammy's just a little annoyed with me right now," I said as we headed into the park. "And don't worry about me getting smacked—I can take care of myself."

"See, there's another joke. You couldn't even take me. And I'm a girl."

"Get outta town," I said. "You're a girl? Is this, like, a recent development? Did I miss something?"

"You miss most things, but you know I'm a girl. That's why you can't even look at me. You're afraid you might melt or something."

"I appreciate your concern for me," I said sarcastically.

"Don't flatter yourself," she replied. "I'm just

against violence in any form. Even if that means you don't get the pounding you deserve."

"I deserve?"

"Yeah. There's no question you deserve it. I mean, think about it. Wapple, Sammy, your soccer coach—"

"Ex–soccer coach," I corrected her.

"Right, your ex–soccer coach," she said. "I wouldn't want to get that wrong. Ex-coach is a lot like ex-friend, isn't it?"

"What's that supposed to mean?"

"You figure it out, Einstein," she said.

"I'm tired today, Annie," I said. "I don't need this. Maybe you should walk on the other side of the street."

"Oh, that's right!" she said, suddenly hopping up and down. She was obviously very excited about something. "Your brother brought Susan home last night, didn't he?"

I stopped walking.

"Where do you *hear* this stuff? I mean, do you know *everything* that goes on in my house, or what?"

"Well, how was she?"

"She was geeky, just like I thought she'd be."

"Did she sit real close to Chuck on the couch? Like were they touching or anything?"

"Man, you're gonna make me puke. What do you care, anyway?"

"I don't. I just like to bug you."

"You're doing a good job."

"Okay, Mitchell, let's get serious for a minute."

I didn't like the sound of that.

"I don't want to get serious," I said.

"You never do, but I have to ask. Are you going mental or something? Look at yourself. You wear the same clothes every day. You're fighting with every teacher you have. Your best friend has had it with you. And of course, you got kicked off the soccer team—"

"Wait." I stopped her dead in her tracks. "I did not get kicked off. I quit. Okay?"

Annie curled her lips into a smirk. "Okay, you quit. Excuse me, please. You got kicked off the first line, then you quit the team. Is that better?"

"Yeah," I snapped. "That's better."

"Well, whatever," she continued. "The thing is, you're a mess. And I think it started a long time before you got kicked off—I mean 'quit'—the soccer team. You've been goofy all fall. What's going on with you?"

"Nothing. Nothing's going on. I'm just being bored to death by people like you. Worry about your own life."

"Everything's fine with my life. That's why I'm having so much fun worrying about yours. It's like a hobby."

"Well, get a new hobby," I said. "Maybe you can collect bugs or something."

We made the last turn and headed up the school sidewalk. I don't think I was ever so happy to see Keller Lake North Middle School.

"Stop, Mitchell," Annie ordered.

I kept walking.

"I mean it, Mitchell, stop. Stop. Stop right now or I'll tell all my friends that you tried to kiss me."

I stopped.

"What?" I asked.

She looked straight into my eyes. The morning sun flashed off her braces.

"I really am worried about you, Mitchell," she said. "You just seem, I don't know . . . you don't seem *happy*."

I looked down and kicked at the dirt.

"Don't worry about me. Nothing's wrong," I said. "Maybe it's just a midlife crisis."

"But you're only thirteen."

"Yeah, but you know me, Annie. I've always been ahead of my time."

9

SLEEPWALKED THROUGH the first part of the day. My head was pounding. Annie had just made it all worse.

Who in the heck was she to start giving me advice? She had a hard enough time with girl stuff, like trying to figure out what shoes she should wear with what shirt and stuff like that.

I mean, stinking-A, who made *her* my personal adviser? *"You don't seem happy"*? Well, Annie was the one who didn't seem *normal*.

I pushed thoughts of Annie aside. I had enough to worry about today.

Like what to do when math class rolled around. I didn't know where to go, so I just headed to Principal Pendleton's office. Mrs. Jenkins was there in her usual spot.

"Aren't you supposed to be in class?" she asked.

"I'm doing an independent study," I said. "I'm researching what it is that everybody does around here. Everybody is especially interested about what you do."

She curled her bright pink upper lip and was about

to say something when Pendleton came out of his office.

"Mitchie!" he boomed. "Get in here."

Mrs. Jenkins gave me a cold sneer as I passed her.

I slumped into the chair in Pendleton's office. "What do I do?" I asked him. "I've never been sent to the slammer before."

"So this is the slammer, huh?" he said. "Well, until you get things patched up with Coach Hendricks, you'll just sit out there with Mrs. Jenkins."

"Oh, man," I said. "Can't I do something else, like scrub the boys' locker room floor with a toothbrush, or do push-ups till I puke? Or anything?"

"Sure," he said. "Work out things with the coach."

"To be honest," I said, "I don't really care if I work things out with him or not. Can't I just get a different math teacher?"

"This isn't a supermarket," said Pendleton. "You don't get to pick your teachers. And I'll tell you why you need to patch things up. Because if you don't pass eighth-grade math, you have to take it all over again. Try and explain that one to your parents."

He had a point. That wouldn't go over well at home *at all*.

Pendleton, all six foot six of him, stared down at me as I pondered this.

"Well," he said. "What do you think you should do?"

"You're the expert," I said. "You tell me what to do and I'll do it."

He smiled. "Just go talk to him."

"I'm not gonna say I'm sorry," I snapped.

"Well, then you may as well just get used to spending time with Mrs. Jenkins."

"But I'm not sorry. What I told him was right. And he knows it."

"Was it right to blow up in class?"

"Maybe not in class . . ."

"Then it's easy," he shot back. "I know the coach well. I don't think he has any problem talking things over. But I know he doesn't like his class disrupted. And I don't blame him. See, Mitchie, it's okay not to agree on something. But there's a time and place for that. And it's not in the middle of class.

"Here's the good news," Pendleton continued. "Many people around here find you amusing—most of the time, that is. But you need to do a better job of knowing when to keep your mouth shut. Get it?"

I didn't answer, but I got it.

"Oh, and one more thing," he said. "Coach Hendricks has detention duty Monday. You'll have all weekend to think about how to persuade him to cut you some slack. Then maybe I'll be able to help get you out from under this."

"Can you get me out of detention today?" I asked, already knowing the answer. "I mean, a Friday afternoon in jail? It's almost cruel and unusual punishment. I bet it's unconstitutional."

"I'm not a miracle worker," Pendleton said. "It'll

be good for you. You could use some good old-fash-ioned detention." He opened a folder on his desk, and that was my signal to leave. I went back out to join the lovely Mrs. Jenkins.

I sat there, totally steamed. I'd been in my share of scrapes, but I'd always been quick enough to avoid detention. I was sure that I'd been responsible for sending a bunch of *other* guys to detention over the years. But me, I'd always been too slippery.

IT WAS TOUGH WATCHING everybody else leave after school, knowing I was stuck there. I took my time before making my way to the very last place I wanted to be right then.

Room 219.

Room 219 is where they send the low-life delin-quent types when they get caught smoking and stuff like that. It's the room where the bad kids go to rot. It's the land of the losers.

And now I was one.

Being a rookie, I had no idea what to do.

You know, when you walk into most middle-school classrooms, it's hard to tell right away what you just walked into. Without scanning the bulletin boards, you probably wouldn't know by looking at the kids if you were in a math class or a history class or whatever.

But you take just one look in 219 after school and you know exactly where you are. This was the sorri-est-looking bunch of dirtballs I'd ever seen in one place. And nobody was doing anything. There were about twenty-five kids in all, from sixth, seventh, and eighth grades. A third of them were passed out with their heads down on the desks. Another third were halfway there—nodding off with their heads bobbing up and down and back and forth like those baseball-player dolls. And the last third, well, they were just sitting there staring off into space. These were the real losers. They weren't even smart enough to sleep.

I walked up to the teacher's desk, where spindly old Mr. Bohabbit was sitting, correcting some papers. He's a history teacher, and everybody always wants to be in his class because he never makes anybody do anything.

I signed my name on the sheet and went to take a desk.

"Hold it," said Bohabbit as he grabbed the clipboard with the sign-in sheet. He pushed his oversize wire-rimmed glasses farther up his nose, then put his face practically right on top of the list. "Evers, Mitchell, is it?"

"That's me," I said.

"Well, Evers, Mitchell. You're late. It's a bad idea to be late to detention. Students who are late to detention usually end up getting more detention."

"Oh, great," I thought. "My first day as a criminal and I'm already screwing up." I decided to turn on the charm.

"I'm sorry, Mr. Bohabbit," I said. "I've never been here before, and I didn't know how everything worked."

"Oh, save it," he said. "Go take a seat, and once you are seated, remain seated. Unless, of course, you have an emergency. Expecting any emergencies this afternoon, Evers, Mitchell?" he asked.

"Well," I said, "you just never know." With that, I started to scope out the seating situation. My plan was to be very low-profile. I didn't want to talk to anyone, and I didn't want anyone talking to me.

The group looked like the cast of a low-budget prison movie. These kids were nasty. I recognized some of them, but there were others I'd never seen before in my life—and I'd been at this school for nearly a year and a half. They must've been detention lifers.

I chose a desk in the middle of the room, close to a group of three girls. My first thought was I'd be safer next to girls. Then I got a closer look. These were some pretty mean-looking females. They were dressed in all black, and two of them had huge pieces of metal—about the size of small Buicks—hanging from their ears. I don't know how they kept their heads up. And each of them had different color hair, colors I'm certain are not found anywhere in nature.

I sat down, pulled *Sports Illustrated* out of my backpack, and buried my head in it. Then I heard a voice.

"Hey, prep boy," whispered the girl closest to me. I looked at her. The bright orange under her eyes played nicely off the electric blue polish on her nails. "What'd you do to get stuck in here, forget to wash your gym clothes?"

I wasn't impressed by this lame attempt at a rip. I put the magazine down slowly and stared at her.

"A teacher was hassling me," I said quietly and carefully. "So I pulled a knife out of my sock and took a couple of seventh-graders hostage."

She was speechless for a second, which I think came somewhat naturally to her. Then a weird look came over her face. Her eyes got real big. "A knife?" she asked. "Wow." Then she turned to her cronies, whispering. She never said another word to me.

The fifty minutes seemed to go on forever.

When the bell rang, I was out of my seat so fast, I was a blur.

This was not how I planned to continue spending my afternoons.

10

As I rounded the corner and started heading up Keller Lane, I prayed that Mom's car wouldn't be in the driveway. That meant Pendleton would have to wait until Monday before he'd get the chance to rat me out. And then I might have a somewhat peaceful weekend.

But I was having absolutely no luck at all. Her car was sitting right there, waiting for me.

I punched in the code on the garage door opener, walked around my dad's fix-up boat, and slipped into the laundry room. Mom's purse was sitting on the washer as usual. I hung up my jacket, grabbed my backpack, and made my way into the house.

I thought my best shot was to just dash up to my room, on the chance that Mom would be on the phone talking to one of her clients. I decided to go for it. I was halfway up the stairs before I heard her.

"Mitchell, is that you?" she called.

I paused, thinking. Maybe it would be better to keep going, slam the door, and fall into bed. If I could just pull my sheets and blankets up over my head, maybe I wouldn't hear anything. Then she called again.

"Mitchell, come here, I need to talk to you."

I decided to get it over with.

I walked into the kitchen. She was still in her good work clothes, but she was sweeping the floor.

"Mitchell, do I really need to come home to this?" she asked.

"Look, Mom," I said. "Before you say anything, let me explain—"

"There's nothing to explain. Your job is to clean up the kitchen before you leave the house in the morning. It's that simple. I'm sick and tired of stepping on crumbs when I walk into the house."

She hadn't talked to Pendleton.

She was just mad about the crumbs on the floor. I'd dodged a bullet!

Then I heard the garage open and a car door slam.

But it was early. It couldn't be my dad already—

"Mitchie! Mitchie, are you home?" he screamed from the garage. He was still yelling when he hit the kitchen. "Mitchie, I want to talk to you!"

My mom looked confused.

"Mitchie, don't I have enough things to worry about right now?" he asked. "Do I really need to get calls from your principal telling me you got kicked out of math class?"

My mom stopped sweeping and looked me. "You got kicked out of math class?" she asked.

"Oh, that's not all," said my dad, slamming down his briefcase. "Mitchie, it appears, has also ticked off half of the rest of his teachers as well."

My mom looked sad. "Oh, Mitchell," was all she could say.

"Dammit, Mitchie," my dad said. "This has got to stop. From now on—"

"Hey, wait a minute," I said, stamping my foot. "Don't I get to say something here?"

"No, Mitchie, you get to say *nothing*." My dad yanked his tie loose before continuing. "This has been going on way too long. You get kicked off the team. You sit up in that room of yours all day and bounce that stupid ball off the wall. You're no fun to be around. Mitchie, what the heck is wrong with you?"

"So that's it," I barked. "You're still mad because I quit the team. Did you ever stop to think it wasn't all my fault? Maybe I had a good reason for quitting. You haven't even asked me what happened or why I did it. If Chuck had quit the team, then you would have understood."

"Chuck would never have quit the team!"

"That's right. Chuck never quits. He's perfect. C'mon, Dad, how do you even know what's going on with me? Between going to school and Chuck's games, you haven't even talked to me in like a year!"

There was silence. Dad just looked at me. Then he stormed out of the kitchen.

My mom turned on me.

"That was totally unfair, Mitchell. Nobody works harder than your father. Now, because you kids are a little older and he thinks you can handle it, he goes back to school so that maybe someday he can find a job he actually enjoys—"

"Mom," I interrupted.

"Wait," she snapped. "I'm not done. And don't think I haven't noticed that you're not thrilled about *me* going back to work, either. Well, Mitchell, I was home for a long time, longer than a lot of mothers. I loved being home. But now I want to work. And because I don't drop everything for you, because I'm not there to clean up your breakfast dishes and fix your after-school snack, you're acting like a baby. You need to grow up and start taking some responsibility, Mitchell."

"Forget it, Mom!" I yelled. "Forget everything! I don't care if you work. Work all the time for all I care."

Just then Shea came in. She had no idea what she was walking into.

"Hey, Mitchie," she said breathlessly. "When are we going to the video store? I think we better go now because—"

"Just a minute, Shea!" I yelled, still trying to think of what to say to Mom.

"But, Mitchie . . ." Shea said.

"Shut *up*, Shea!"

"Mitchie!" she whined.

"Just shut up, Shea!" I screamed. "Don't you get it? I don't want to watch that stupid movie!"

Then everything just stopped. Shea looked up at me in a daze, like somebody had just punched her in the gut.

I had never talked to her like that.

Never.

My mom didn't know what to say either.

After a few seconds, I saw the color come back into Shea's cheeks and her eyes start to swell up and turn red. Then the tears came, and she cocked her head slightly, looking at me like she didn't even know me. Finally she ran off toward her room.

I didn't know what to do.

"Great job, Mitchell," said my mother. "That was just perfect."

I started toward the back door; then I stopped. Then I started again, and stopped again. I stood there for another second. Then I slammed my open hand on the wall and finally ran off after my sister.

When I got to her room, her door was shut. I knocked.

"Shea," I called through the door. "I'm sorry."

"Go away," came the reply.

"I mean it, Shea. I'm really sorry."

"Go away, Mitchie! I don't want to talk to you! Ever!"

"Come on, Shea."

"Go away!"

I walked slowly across the hall, went into my room, slammed the door, and lay down on my bed.

Then I buried my head under a pillow and cried like a stinking baby.

I WAS ONLY ABOUT four, so I don't remember exactly what it was like when Shea was born, but my mom said I was the proudest big brother in the world.

At the hospital, I'd march all the visitors down to

67

the nursery and point at Shea, reminding everyone that now there were two big brothers. Chuck was still a big brother, but now I was a big brother too.

When Grandma Evers asked me about having a new sister around the house, I told her that Shea was going to live at the hospital, but that she'd come over to visit us once in a while. I guess my grandma thought that was pretty funny. Hey, I was four. What did I know?

Shea started walking pretty early, and Mom says that from the very beginning, she'd follow me around like a dog. When she was two, I'd safety-pin a towel to her sleepers like a cape and call her Super Baby. When she was three, she went through about a year when she'd only sleep with me. I'd read a book to her every night, and then she'd fall asleep on my pillow. Whenever my mom or dad tried to move her, she'd say, "No, Mitchie's bed, Mitchie's bed."

In fact, Shea was the one who started the whole "Mitchie" thing. Besides "Mama" and "Dada," Shea's first real word was my name. Only she couldn't say "Mitchell," so it came out "Mitchie." No one called me that until she did. It sounds like a baby name, but I don't mind. Shea gave me that name.

It's one thing to make your mom and your dad and your big brother and your best friend feel crummy. You kind of hope they're smart enough to figure out what's going on.

But it's something else when you dump on a nine-year-old, especially when she thinks you're just about the neatest thing on earth. Even when I quit the team, Shea was on my side. She said, "You should just start your own team, and then smack those other guys." She didn't get it, but she was absolutely certain that I was right.

Now I'd let her down, big-time. I had just accomplished the impossible. I'd made Shea—for the first time ever—hate her big brother.

And it was the lowest feeling I ever had in my life.

I STAYED IN my room the rest of the night, going downstairs only after I heard everybody go up to bed. I made myself a quick sandwich and ran back to my room.

I tried to watch TV, but I couldn't find anything interesting. I even tried to look through some old comics, but that didn't help either. Mostly I just lay in bed and stared at the star chart I had pinned to the ceiling.

I was wishing I was somewhere else—or *someone* else.

So I thought about that for a while too. But it hurt my brain to think about it too hard, so I finally just drifted off to sleep.

11

I WOKE UP EARLY Saturday morning and looked outside. No change. Cold and gray.

And no snow.

I snuck downstairs, found myself a bagel, spread some cream cheese on it, washed it down with apple juice, and threw my dishes in the machine.

I put on my heavy coat and my boots, and grabbed a blanket. Then I headed out the door. It was only about eight o'clock.

As I walked along the lake, I was thinking about November. I have mixed feelings about it. Daylight savings time is over, so you have to eat dinner in the dark, and I really hate that. It used to be kind of okay because it meant soccer season was over and I could just come home after school and talk to my mom and eat cookies and junk like that. But then I quit the soccer team, and Mom went out and got a job, so it wasn't the same anymore.

But then there's the other part of November. Thanksgiving is in November and that's my favorite holiday. I know that's weird. Most guys like Christmas because of the presents and stuff. Don't get me wrong, I'm a big Christmas guy too.

But Thanksgiving is special. Now, I don't say this to a lot of people, because I don't want anyone to think I'm some kind of baby wimp. But Thanksgiving is about family and being together and being thankful, and all that other stuff. I know that sounds kind of lame—and it probably doesn't sound like me.

But it's really how I want things to be.

And there's one more big reason I like November. The snow.

When November starts, everything is gray and gloomy. All the leaves are gone and the trees look like witches with spindly, twisted arms and fingers reaching up to a cold, dark sky. You can look right through the trees on the south end of Keller Lake and see the houses on the other side. It's as if that big forest where we hide in the summer just morphs into nothing.

But then the snow comes.

The first couple of snowfalls are usually fat and wet and the snow clings to trees and houses like frosting on shredded wheat. The trees aren't scary looking anymore. They're clean and new. In fact, they're magic. At least that's what I always used to think, and sometimes still do.

November snow usually comes before the lake freezes. The shore turns white and the snow lands silently as it's swallowed up by the lake. For a long time, when the year's first snow would come, Chuck and me would wrap Shea up tight, drag her out across the park, and show her the snow falling into the lake.

We'd take off her mitten and hold out her hand so she could catch the flakes. She wouldn't say a word, just look at us, kind of wrinkle her nose, and then shiver and grin.

"Take off my boots," she yelled once when she was about four. "I want to walk in the snow. I want to feel snow in my toes." So we did, and she shrieked as her tiny bare feet touched the icy snow. Then we quickly dried them and put her boots back on. When we got home, she ran into the house with a huge smile, peeled off her boots, jacket, and snow pants, and yelled to Mom that she had just felt snow between her toes. Mom looked at Chuck and me like we were child abusers. Shea said, "Don't be mad, Mommy. They showed me how snow feels between my toes. I didn't know that before."

Last year we missed the first snowfall. It snuck in when we weren't paying attention. Chuck, as usual, was off doing something extremely important and I was just too tired to get out of bed. Shea tried to get me to wake up and get dressed, but I didn't feel like it. She cried.

It bothered me later that I'd made her cry.

I KEPT WALKING TOWARD the beach. Even without the snow I love the park early on a cold morning. I saw one jogger, but that was about it. I went over to our touch football field. It looked sad and empty. Then I walked over to the lifeguard chairs. I climbed up one, but the wind was blowing hard off the frozen lake, so I got down in a hurry.

Finally I made my way over to the slide in the little kids' playground.

It isn't the greatest slide in the world. It's metal and it's slow. It achieved great fame about four years ago when Sammy's neighbor Martin did the unthinkable—he touched his tongue to the metal railing going up one side of the ladder. It was about eight degrees outside, and of course his tongue froze right to it. I thought we were gonna have to call 911, but then, like an idiot, he yanked it off. It came loose, but there was blood all over.

Anyway, this slide is special because at the top of the ladder there's a little fort where you can sit and look out over the lake and the neighborhood. It's not real high, but when I was a kid, I thought I could see the whole world from up there.

I laid out the blanket, knowing the metal would be very cold. I sat there and just looked out over the lake.

Nothing was moving. The wind had died down and the trees were perfectly still.

The lake looked especially eerie because it was frozen solid but not at all smooth. I could see little waves and ridges frozen right in. It looked like the surface of some far-off planet, kind of like you see in those lame science fiction movies that Sammy and Shea like. Usually you can't see the ice because by the time it's cold enough to freeze, it's covered with snow. And that makes the lake look fresh and clean.

But not today. Today it looked like a frozen wasteland. And I felt trapped in the bad part of November.

We needed the snow—snow that would make everything new again.

I didn't really know why I was there. I mean, I don't know what I expected to see or learn. So I just sat and shivered.

Suddenly I heard a clanging against the ladder. What other idiot would be out here in this weather?

Then I heard her.

"Geez, Mitchell, you're not gonna jump or anything, are you? Should I call the police?"

Annie.

Her head popped up over the side.

"C'mon, give me a hand here, will ya?" she said.

I reached over and she handed me a Thermos and a bag.

"Hot chocolate," she said. "I was hoping I'd find you before you were frozen solid and I'd have to chip you out of here with an ice pick."

"How'd you know I was here?" I asked, handing her the Thermos after she sat down on the blanket.

"I saw it on CNN," she said. "Big headlines: Mitchell Evers located freezing his butt off on an old metal slide. Update at ten o'clock."

"No, really," I said. "How'd you know I was here?"

"Well, think about it. You have to walk past my house to get here. I just happened to be up and I saw you out the window. When I saw the blanket, I knew you were coming here. You're really not that hard to figure out, Mitchell."

Annie and I had spent a lot of time on this slide. It was our launching pad to space. It was the bridge of our aircraft carrier. It was our minivan going to California. And it was our observatory, looking up at the stars.

"You know what, Mitchell?" Annie said.

"No, what?" I replied.

"It's really cold up here. Where's that hot chocolate?"

She pulled out two big plastic mugs from the bag and poured us each a steaming cup of hot chocolate.

"You know, this isn't that instant stuff, Mitchell. This is the real deal, Hershey's syrup and milk. The best."

"Yeah," I said, "but where are the marshmallows?"

"They're for wimps," Annie answered.

Neither of us said anything for while. We just sat and sipped cocoa.

"Hendricks kicked me out of math," I said finally.

"I saw that on CNN too," she said.

"Sammy's still not talking to me."

"Everybody knows that."

"I said unbelievably stupid things to my mom and dad last night."

"I didn't know that, but it sounds like something you'd do."

"And after that, I yelled at Shea."

"She's tough. She'll bounce back."

We were quiet for a while.

Annie broke the silence. "So, what are you gonna do about everything?"

"I might join the Marines," I said. "Or maybe become a foreign exchange student, someplace real far away. Maybe I could be a missionary in Africa."

I turned and looked into Annie's eyes.

"Annie, I've really screwed things up this time. I know I'm only thirteen, but maybe I've already used up all my free passes."

"Oh, geez, quit acting like it's the end of the world," she said. "C'mon, you're just a kid. You're supposed to screw up. Other than me, there are very few perfect people in this world."

"Yeah, but it's just—"

"It's just nothing. It's part of the deal. Remember two years ago, when you had that awful summer soccer season? You couldn't make a play to save your life. You'd sit up here and tell me you were the worst guy on the team, that you'd never be any good. Remember all that?"

"Yeah, so?"

"Well, think about it, you blockhead. Did you forget how to play the game? Did you become a horrible soccer player overnight? Or was it something else?"

I still didn't get it.

"Duh, Mitchell," Annie went on. "Do you think maybe it was just a slump?"

"A slump?" I repeated.

"A slump, Mitchell. It was just a slump. Everybody goes through them. That summer you weren't getting any breaks. The ball was bouncing funny off your foot and you were missing your shots. But you came back and played great in the play-offs, remember?"

"What does that have to do with—"

"What do I have to do here—draw you a picture?" She straightened up and tugged at her cap.

"You're in another slump, Mitchell," she said. "You're missing your shots. The ball's bouncing funny off your foot. I mean, it may be like the worst slump ever in the history of the universe, because your friends and family and teachers all want to ship you off to Alaska. But it's still just a slump. You can pull out of it. There's no reason to jump off a bridge."

"Okay, Yoda," I said. "So how do I get out of this slump?"

"How'd ya get out of the last one? You worked with Chuck more. You went down and took about a billion shots off the board. Maybe you ate better. You got proper rest. Basically, you just worked your way out of it."

"Oh, so I'll just go kick the ball around and every-thing'll be okay, is that what you're telling me? Listen, I don't think kicking the ball around is going to help much. Especially now. My soccer career is over, remember?"

"Is that what it is? You think your soccer career is over? You're thirteen and you're all washed up? Forever?"

"Well, since I'm not on the team, it doesn't look too good," I said.

"You are so incredibly stupid sometimes, Mitchell," Annie said. "Hendricks bumped you off the starting line so you're just gonna give up?"

"What's the point? I have no chance of making varsity next year now, not after what happened."

Annie shook her head. "Well, moron, what about the year after that? And the two years after that? Even if you don't make varsity next year, you'd still have three years left. Geez, Mitchell, I don't think you're seeing the big picture here. What's so important about making varsity next year?"

I got up on my knees and looked her in the eye. "All I've ever thought about since I started playing was making the varsity team as a ninth-grader. Otherwise, it just doesn't matter."

"Then do it," she said. "Just shut up and do it. I don't know exactly what it's going to take to get you out of this slump. But I do know nothing's going to happen as long as you sit up here all bug-eyed, staring out into nothing."

I thought about that for a minute.

"So I shouldn't run off and join the Marines?" I asked.

"I didn't say that," she shot back. "That'd probably be a good idea for all of us. It sure would be a heck of a lot easier."

We sat there quietly for another few minutes, finishing our cocoa, looking out over the ice.

"Annie," I said finally, "if you're so brilliant, tell me this: Why can't things ever just stay the same? I mean, why can't things be like they used to be? Like when we'd sit up here and pretend we were flying off to Jupiter?"

"Sorry to burst your bubble, Mitchell, but sitting up here and pretending we're junior astronauts is not how I want to spend the rest of *my* life."

"Yeah, but we had great times, didn't we?"

"Sure we did," said Annie. "And we had great times in kindergarten eating paste, too. But I don't think I want to repeat that experience."

She turned to me and pulled her hat down even tighter. Her cheeks were big and pink, and her strawberry hair was twisted between her scarf and her hat, making it go in about six different directions.

"Mitchell, here's a bulletin: Things change. Moms get jobs. School gets harder. Soccer coaches get ticked off. Little boys have to grow up. It's all part of some cosmic plan."

"I'm not a little boy."

She let out one of her Annie laughs, honking like one of the Keller Lake geese.

"Oh, that's right," she said. "You just act like one. Mitchell, has anybody died? Has your dad been sent off to prison? Are you being forced at gunpoint to watch infomercials? No. So snap out of it. Quit acting like the whole world's out to get you. The truth is, you're just not that important."

She sat back, took one last long drink of her hot chocolate, and rearranged her hat and scarf. Then suddenly, as if she was late for a meeting, she got up, dumped the drips out of her mug, grabbed mine, loaded them in the bag, and started down the ladder.

"I gotta go, Mitchell," she said. "It's way too cold today to be sitting on top of a freezing metal slide. Only a loser would do something so incredibly lame."

And like a diver going under the water, her head disappeared below the side rail, and she was gone.

I STAYED UP THERE for a few minutes longer.

Annie was right. Things did change.

I'd already pretty much figured that out, even though I didn't want to admit it. It might have taken the entire fall, but I was finally getting that.

But the idea that it was all just a temporary deal—a slump—that was news to me. I'd just spent the last few months thinking my brother was *always* going to be a jerk, my teachers were *always* going to be idiots, my mom and dad were *always* going to be too busy for me . . . and that I was *never* gonna play soccer again. And I'd never even considered the possibility that maybe, just maybe, I could change some of that. Maybe change all of it.

But as I sat there, I still couldn't figure out how. So I tried to think of one big thing I could do, something that might get everything else going in the right direction.

And the answer that came was as clear and sharp as the cold, wintry air that was stinging my cheeks. It was time to end my soccer retirement. It was time to get back in the game.

Annie thought I should play even if I had no chance of making varsity as a ninth-grader. But not me. I had always had a plan, and if I was actually going to make a soccer comeback now, it was going to be so I could play varsity next year as a ninth-grader.

I just had to.

And if I could pull it off, it would be the greatest comeback of all time.

As for Shea and my mom and Dad and Sammy— well, I had to fix all that stuff too. But those answers weren't coming as easy.

Actually, the more I thought about it, the more I knew that none of it—including the soccer—would be easy.

12

WHEN I GOT HOME from the park, I decided to strap on my old Rollerblades and take a spin around the neighborhood. I figured it wasn't too early to start on my soccer conditioning program.

At first I was freezing. My skates felt tight on my feet, and my lungs burned, and my thighs hurt. But after a few minutes, I started to feel better. I hadn't worked up a really good sweat since I quit the team. It felt good to get loose again.

I took the long way up Keller Lane and headed toward the lake. I thought I'd skate along the lake path, even though the wind was whipping across, making every breath painful.

I jumped the patch of grass where the path hit Park Place and headed up toward County Road 42, the closest busy street to my house.

I was working pretty good by now. My strides were getting longer and I was finding a good pace. I'd unzipped my jacket a bit, and I took off my sweaty hat and stuffed it into my pocket.

I went up 42 until I got to Walgreens. By then I'd been skating pretty hard for almost an hour, and I needed a break. I had a couple of bucks in my pocket, so I decided to go inside and get something to eat.

I was thinking that since this was my first real workout since soccer, I'd get a granola bar and probably some Gatorade. You know, something healthy that would replenish the nutrients I lost Rollerblading. I pondered this a moment or two.

Then I grabbed a Mountain Dew and some Hostess Twinkies and headed toward the cash register.

In the checkout line, I started looking at the sleazy newspapers. One said the spirit of Elvis was taking over the body of the Queen of England.

Because I was so interested in broadening my mind, I didn't notice until too late that Sammy and his dad were at the head of the line.

Our eyes met for a second before we each turned away. Then I heard Sammy's dad say, "Hey, look, Sam. There's Mitchie." Sam kind of gave me a limp wave and I kind of nodded back. I could tell from the look on Sammy's dad's face that he had no idea what was going on.

They paid for their stuff and headed toward the magic door. That's what Shea calls it, because she doesn't get how it opens without anybody touching it. Anyway, I hesitated for a second; then I plopped my junk on the counter behind me and decided to go after him.

But I got there too late. By the time I reached the parking lot, their car was already pulling out and heading for the street. Sammy saw me, but he turned away real quick.

"Go ahead," I thought. "Don't even give me a chance."

I went back inside, got my stuff, and paid for it. I was still sweaty and it was too cold to sit outside, so I just crammed myself in the little area between the inside and outside doors and drank my Dew and ate my Twinkies.

People had to kind of step around me to get through, and after a few minutes, I started to feel like some kind of bum, sitting there all alone eating junk food out of a paper bag. I took one last bite out of my second Twinkie, slammed down one last swig of my Dew, and hit the road.

13

SHEA SPENT THE ENTIRE weekend avoiding me, knowing that it was bugging the heck out of me. I even heard her tell Ali—her goofy little best friend—that I wasn't around because I was undergoing some kind of experimental treatment for emotional problems.

My mom and dad were pretty quiet. None of us knew what to say, so none of us said much of anything. I was waiting for the hammer to fall—some kind of punishment for my getting kicked out of math and their getting a call from the principal. But it never came. I guess they figured getting detention was bad enough.

My mom went out and got Shea's video, and they watched it together. I thought about walking in and watching it with them, but somehow I knew I didn't deserve it. Chuck didn't say a thing to me, either. I could tell he was ticked. He doesn't like it when I give our parents grief.

So I tried to lie low. I made sure my stuff was picked up and I kept out of everyone's way.

I wanted to work things out with everybody but I really wasn't sure how to do it. I could also tell they were still a bit too hot. My gut told me to wait awhile.

When Monday rolled around, I was almost glad to be going back to school.

I took the regular path to Sammy's. I knew he wouldn't be there, but I'd decided to just keep going to his house every morning until he figured out I wasn't going to go away.

It was the coldest day of the year so far, but since it was still just November, I wasn't wearing a hat. This may have been especially stupid, because my hair was still wet. It was really bright, with the sun working its way down through the crystal air. It's always colder when it's clear, and I knew it was gonna stay cold. Of course, it just kills me when it's that cold and there's no snow. It just seems like everything's out of whack.

When I got to Sammy's, Mrs. Travis came out wearing her bathrobe.

"Sam already left," she said before I even asked.

As I turned to go, I heard her mumble something else.

"What?" I asked.

"I said," she replied, adjusting her glasses and pulling her robe tight to keep out the cold November wind, "what's up with you two?"

"What do you mean?" I asked, knowing exactly what she meant.

She shrugged, but I couldn't tell if it was because she was ticked at me, or if she was just freezing.

"Oh, come on, Mitchie," she said. "Sam didn't wait for you again, and he hasn't mentioned you for a couple of days. Sam's dad said you two saw each other at Walgreens and didn't even say a word to each other."

I readjusted my backpack and kicked at the dirt. "I guess I really ticked him off this time. I guess I finally pushed him over the edge."

"Well, straighten it out," Mrs. Travis snapped, turning to go inside. "I'm tired of him moping around the house."

So Sam was moping around too. Interesting.

Maybe he wasn't totally through with old Mitchie after all.

THE MORNING SEEMED to drag on forever. I tried my best to stay awake during science, and somehow I managed. About halfway through, Harris asked me a pretty tough question and I shocked him by having a decent answer.

"What, Mr. Evers?" he asked. "No clever comeback? Maybe you haven't recovered from a wild weekend?"

I didn't look up.

"Yeah, that's it," I said.

I tried to pay attention during my afternoon classes, but I was thinking ahead to detention, when I'd have my chance to talk to Hendricks.

I was pretty much in a daze the rest of the day, but I was starting to focus as I headed for room 219. In fact, my head was getting real clear.

Coach was sitting at the desk. I walked in and wrote my name on the sign-in sheet.

"Hi, Coach," I said.

"Good afternoon," said the coach.

"Uh, Coach?"

"What, Mitchie?"

"Do you think in a few minutes, I mean after you get everybody set here, we can talk about some stuff?"

He'd been expecting this.

"Yeah," he said. "I think we can. Just sit down and I'll come find you."

I nodded and took a seat next to my new friends from Friday, the friends with the very bright hair.

I hadn't been there long when the coach came down and told me to follow him into the hall. Like Friday, there was no need to worry about a riot from the inmates. They were all zombies.

Coach leaned against the wall. "So?" he asked.

I took a deep breath. "Here's the deal. I want to get back into math. I thought about what happened, and I shouldn't have blown up at you during class."

"Is that an apology?"

"For blowing up in class, it is."

"But not for what you said?"

"I don't know," I said. "I still don't think it was fair for you to treat me crummy in class just because you didn't like what I was doing on the field."

Coach Hendricks reached up and scratched his thin blond hair. "Didn't we already have this conversation?" he asked. "I try real hard to separate the field from the classroom. But I'm human. You disappointed me, Mitchie. Not the way you played, but the way you reacted every time I tried to tell you something."

He continued. "But none of that matters right now. The problem now is math. And here's the only deal I'm willing to make. I'll let you back in tomorrow—which I think is being very generous—but I don't want to hear one word from you. I don't even want to hear you breathe. You can ask an appropriate question or provide an answer when I'm asking for one. But other than that, you're like a hologram. We'll all be able to see you, but it won't seem real, because for the first time in his life, Mitchie Evers is just going to listen and keep his mouth shut. Is that clear?"

I was quiet for a second. I didn't want to look defeated. But I knew I was.

"It's clear," I said quietly.

"Fine," Hendricks said. "Now go back and sit down with your fellow inmates."

"One more thing," I said.

"Is this an appropriate question?" he asked.

"Yeah," I said. "I think so."

"Go ahead."

I took another deep breath.

"Am I gonna be in a real jam with soccer next year?"

"Oh," he said. "You're thinking about playing again?"

Now he was really working me.

"Well, not if I don't have a chance. Not if people are gonna keep talking about what happened this year."

"That's a great attitude, Mitchie," Hendricks said. "You're still trying to do everything on *your* terms."

"I didn't mean it that way," I said. "I know it's going to be tough, and I'm willing to do everything I need to. I just don't want to go through it all if nobody's going to give me a chance."

"Believe it or not, Mitchie, you're not that special. No one has the time to *try* to make your life miserable." Then he sighed real big.

"Look," he said. "Quitting the team in the middle of the season is not something coaches forget about. But some of us do believe in giving people second chances."

I perked up. "You do?"

"What are we going to do, Mitchie? Say you can never go out for Keller Lake sports again because you quit *one* time?"

He paused, then gave me a big-time serious look.

"Mitchie, you shouldn't have quit," he said. "You let your team down, and you let me down. But people make mistakes. Everyone makes mistakes."

He stopped and stared at the ceiling. It looked like he was thinking about something and he wasn't sure if he should tell me about it or not. Then finally he got back to me.

"Here's one for you," he said. "When I was a junior in high school, I lived way up north, not around here. I was, without a doubt, the best player on my high-school baseball team. I was a great shortstop. I had the range, a big-time arm, and I could hit, too. The whole package. But my coach decided I should play left field because we had a senior who wanted to play shortstop. I was better, and everyone knew it.

"Well, I just moped around and acted like a jerk. I didn't hustle, I was lazy in the field, and I didn't run out ground balls. Finally my coach benched me, and about halfway through the season, I quit."

"You *quit*?" I asked.

"You bet," he said. "After all, I should've been starting at short, right?"

"Right," I answered.

"Wrong," the coach shot back. "See, Mitchie, the other guy was a good, solid shortstop, but he had a hard time judging fly balls in the outfield. I was a better shortstop, but he couldn't play outfield. By putting him at short and me in left, the coach could put both of us in the lineup. We had a much stronger team that way. Oh, and another thing. The other guy was a senior. He'd worked really hard. It was his last year. He deserved it. I was just a junior. I had another whole year to play."

"Did you come back for your senior year?"

"I almost didn't," he said. "Finally my dad talked me into it. But it was hard. I barely played at all the first four or five games, but by about midseason, I was the starting shortstop, and I had a pretty good year."

"So everything worked out," I said.

"I suppose so," Coach answered. "But I always wonder what would have happened if I'd just stayed around and played left field my junior year."

"What do you mean?" I asked.

"Well, I missed a lot of games—games that I never got back. My dad still thinks it cost me a college scholarship."

"Really?" I said.

"Who knows?" Hendricks said, pulling off his glasses and rubbing his eyes. "One thing is sure, though, I had *no* chance after missing half of both my junior and senior years."

He was quiet for a minute.

"But you should be okay," he said. "That is, if you've learned anything from all this. You've got to understand, Mitchie—a coach has to think about everyone on the team."

"So, am I gonna have a tough time with the coach next year?" I asked.

He played with his glasses, twirling them around. "Coach Eubanks is a reasonable guy. Don't expect him to get on his knees and thank you for coming out again. He knows you quit this season, and he's not going to make it easy for you. He doesn't have a lot of patience. But if you work hard and keep your mouth shut—kind of like you need to do in math class— you'll do fine."

"What if I want to do better than fine?" I asked.

Hendricks got a funny look on his face. "What does that mean?" he said.

I blurted it out. "Do I have any chance at making varsity next year?"

He looked stunned.

"I don't know what to say to that," he said. "It's really not even worth discussing at this point. First you need to worry about impressing Coach Eubanks."

He put his glasses back on and ran his hand through his hair again. "All right," he said. "You better get back inside with the rest of the prisoners. I guess I'll see you in class tomorrow."

"That's it?" I asked. It was just too easy—maybe he was feeling a bit guilty. "I'm back just like that?"

"What did you think I was going to do?" he said. "You didn't kill anyone. I'm a reasonable guy. But don't screw up again."

I headed back to the classroom, but then I stopped. I turned to Coach Hendricks.

"Uh, Coach," I said, barely looking up. "What about varsity next year?"

"Mitchie," he said, "one step at a time."

"But it's important."

"I'm sure it is," he said. "One step at a time."

14

I RAN HOME AFTER detention, strapped on my blades, and headed out the door. As I skated, I thought about Hendricks. I wondered if maybe I shouldn't have brought up all that stuff about varsity. But I knew I had to.

I was back home in forty-five minutes. On the counter was a note from my mom:

> Mitchell:
> I'm picking up Shea from school and we're going shopping. We'll be home around 6:30 or 6:45. Dad has his last class tonight and Chuck's going to Susan's, so it's just the three of us. Go ahead and eat if you're hungry. Otherwise, wait for Shea and me and I'll fix us something. Don't make a mess.
>
> Mom

I was starving. I started rifling through the kitchen. Since my mom had gone back to work, there was never any good food around.

I looked in the bread drawer, thinking maybe I could make some toast or something. But there was nothing there.

All that was left of the Oreos was that black crumbly junk on the bottom of the wrapper. I licked that off and threw it away. It wasn't enough. I was having some serious hunger pangs. I found like six different open boxes of crackers, but every single one was stale. It was pathetic.

The only thing I found in the cupboard that looked halfway decent was a jar of spaghetti sauce. I looked on the next shelf up and I saw box of spaghetti noodles.

Then I thought, did I really want to go through all that just to make some lame spaghetti? I'd probably just be better off waiting for Mom and Shea to come home. It would be easier. Even though I'd seen my mom do it a billion times, I'd never really made spaghetti myself.

But then I started to think . . . All of a sudden, I smelled opportunity.

I ran back to the refrigerator and swung open the door. Yes! There were some of those instant roll things in the tube. I yanked open the freezer. Perfect, a half pound of hamburger. In this incredibly empty kitchen, I had everything I needed to make supper for me, Mom, and Shea.

How many times had my mom yelled at me lately for not doing my share around the house? Selfish Mitchie was gonna turn some heads by making a nice dinner. Here was a chance to earn some big-time points. I had about an hour to pull this off. I could do it.

But I didn't know where to start.

I decided to set the table first. I ran into the hall-way and pulled the big white tablecloth out of the linen closet. There was a bunch of junk on the dining room table—letters and papers and stuff. I scooped it all up and threw it on the desk in the living room.

I looked at the clock and suddenly it hit me that I was taking too much time. I could set the table *after* I started cooking the stuff.

I found a big frying pan and dumped in the burger. It was frozen like a brick, so I turned the burner on high. Then I pulled out the rolls: "Heat oven to 400" it said on the package. So I did. Then I peeled off the wrapper so the dough could pop out. Only I ripped open the tube a little too hard. The dough *did* pop out—right onto the floor.

"Stinking-A!" I screamed, picking up the dough. Little bits of dirt were stuck to one side. At first I thought I'd better dump the dough. But it wouldn't be a special dinner without fresh rolls.

So I stuck the raw dough in the sink and hosed it off with the sprayer. Who was gonna know?

That's when the smoke detector went off.

I hadn't even noticed the smoke coming out of the pan from the burning meat. I snatched the frying pan handle and yanked it off the stove. I nearly dropped it, but I held on. I got a broom and used the handle to poke the button on the detector and stop the noise, but not before it gave me permanent ear damage.

Then I took a quick look around.

The tablecloth was only covering half the dining room table because I'd put it on the wrong way. I didn't have any of the plates or forks or junk out. Dough was lying in the sink. Bits of hamburger meat and the rolls' tube were scattered across the floor. And I was standing there holding a pan of burnt meat.

"This was a big-time bad idea," I thought. I had only about twenty-five minutes until Shea and Mom would hit the door.

I knew what I had to do. I put the pan down and picked up the phone.

"Man, I'm glad you're home," I said to Annie.

"Excuse me," she said. "I believe we have a bad connection."

"Quit messing with me," I snapped. "I need you over here right away!"

"What, is something wrong?" she asked.

"No," I whined. "But you gotta get over here now! I've, uh, got a slight problem."

"Call nine-one-one," she said. I swear she was laughing.

"C'mon, Annie," I begged. "I'll make it worth something."

"What?" she asked.

"Just get over here!" I yelled, and slammed down the phone.

Within about twelve seconds, Annie came strolling through the back door.

"Geez," she said, throwing her jacket over a chair. "You didn't tell me it was a cooking emergency." She looked around, carefully sizing up the joint. "Why is there dough in the sink? And why does it smell like smoke in here?"

I explained everything to her. She thought it was pretty funny that I would even try to cook dinner.

"You know," I said, trying to find a cookie sheet to put the dough on, "I *have* cooked before. It's not like I'm a total idiot."

"Yeah, right," she said, scraping the burnt hamburger out of the pan. "Maybe you've made microwave popcorn or something. That's not cooking. Okay, we'll need a new pan for the hamburger and a pot to boil the water in for the spaghetti. Then go in and finish setting that table. And turn that tablecloth around. Mitchell, you are *so* lame."

I kind of wanted to tell her off then, but instead I found myself watching her from the dining room. She really knew what she was doing. In what seemed like one motion she got the dough in the oven, put the rest of the burger in the new pan, and put water in a big pot to boil.

"You got any vegetables?" she called.

"We don't need vegetables, do we?"

"Don't be ridiculous, Mitchell. You've got to have vegetables."

I told her there was corn in the freezer.

"Put it in one of the glass pans down there and stick it in the microwave," I said, gesturing to the correct cupboard. "About three and a half minutes on high."

"Oh, really?" she said. "Thank you for telling me that, Mitchell. I thought maybe you served the corn frozen."

After she had everything started, she pulled plates and glasses from the cupboard. When I had figured out the tablecloth, I just kind of stood around and watched. "Where's the silverware, you moron?" Annie asked.

I pointed to the drawer.

"Do you think you can handle the knives and forks?" she asked.

I nodded.

"Well, then, do it," she barked. "I gotta put the noodles in."

I kept watching her as I put down the knives and forks. She was really pretty good. After she slid the noodles carefully into the boiling water, she opened the jar of spaghetti sauce and dumped it over the burger. Then she found a pot holder and checked on the rolls in the oven.

"Are you gonna have any dessert?" she asked.

"I don't think so," I said. "Hey, what side does the fork go on?"

"Left side," she said. "What about dessert? You've got no salad, no dessert. Just spaghetti and corn?"

"Don't forget the rolls," I said.

"Yeah, you've got rolls," she said. "That makes it all *very* festive. Hey, do you have something to put these noodles in to drain? And pour the milk and put the glasses in the refrigerator so it stays cold."

While I was doing that, she issued another order. "Okay, these rolls will be ready in about ten minutes, and so will the noodles."

"Sir! Yes sir!" I said, snapping to attention.

"All you need to do is pour out the water and rinse the noodles. Start the corn when Shea and your mom walk in. Then it'll be nice and hot. You know how to put the spaghetti sauce on the noodles, don't you?"

I started going spastic. "No," I said with my tongue hanging out of my mouth, and my eyes rolling. "I'm a moron, remember? I don't know *what* to do."

"Well," she said. "You *are* the guy who washed off the bread dough in the sink and started the hamburger on fire."

"It never actually started on *fire*," I said.

"You were lucky." She wiped her hands with the dish towel. "My work here is done. Didn't you promise to pay me or something?"

I looked at the clock. "Yeah," I said. "We'll work something out. But you have to get outta here. They're gonna walk in at any minute—"

Just as I said that, I heard the garage door open.

"Quick," I said urgently. "Go out the back."

But it was too late. Just as Annie was grabbing her jacket, Shea ran in from the laundry room. She was carrying her backpack on one shoulder.

She slipped off her shoes, then got about halfway through the kitchen before she stopped.

"Why are you here, Annie?" she asked. "And what smells so good?"

"Rolls," I said, acting kind of cool. "*Fresh* rolls."

"Shea," called my mom sternly as she walked in. "Don't dump your shoes right in front of the door. I nearly tripped over them." Then she she looked up from the mail she was carrying. "Oh, hi, Annie. How are you?"

Annie moved toward the back door. Her face was red. "I'm fine, Mrs. Evers. I'm just leaving."

My mom gave me a weird look. Then she saw the spaghetti on the stove.

A goofy smile came over her face and she turned to me and asked, "Mitchell, what gives?"

"Well, uh—" I began before being interrupted by Annie.

"Mrs. Evers," she blurted out. "Mitchell here decided to make dinner for you and Shea tonight, but, uh, he didn't have any corn, so he called me and I brought it over. See you later."

"That's right, Mom," I added. "No corn. Thanks for the corn, Annie."

Annie started out the door.

"Hold it, Annie," said my mom. "We're out of almost everything, but I know we had corn." She paused for a second. "Annie, did you help him with all this?"

We were busted.

"Well," Annie said, "I might have helped a little bit."

I couldn't stand it anymore.

"Okay, Mom, she did it all," I confessed. "It was my idea, but then I practically set fire to the hamburger and dropped the dough and I didn't know what to do, so I called Annie. I was just trying to do something nice, and it really does look pretty good, so let's just eat."

My mom came over and touched my face. "That

101

was very nice, Mitchell. I just got done telling your sister that the last thing I wanted to do tonight was cook. Thank you."

Then she turned to Annie.

"But you have to stay for dinner too," she said. "After all, you cooked it."

Annie looked at me, knowing I didn't want her to stay.

"Well, thanks, Mrs. Evers. I'll just call my mom." She shot me a triumphant little smile. I guess she got her payment.

"Did you really set the hamburger on fire?" Shea asked. "Like, did you do it on purpose? Did you call the fire department?"

"It was just a small cooking incident," I said. "Nobody got hurt."

I brought out another plate for Annie and my mom served up the spaghetti. Annie sat across the table from me, on the same side as Shea. But Shea couldn't leave things alone.

"No, Annie, you have to go sit next to Mitchie," she said. "When Chuck brings his girlfriend home for dinner, they sit on the same side."

Annie giggled, but at least she had the good sense not to move.

"She's *not* my girlfriend," I said.

My mom's eyes flashed, and Shea cracked up, laughing. I didn't dare look at Annie.

But then I cracked up too.

15

BY THE TIME MATH rolled around the next day, I made sure I was early. The Weasel, knowing I was on top-level probation, was doing his best to get me to laugh. But I remembered what Hendricks had told me.

Be a hologram.

And I was. I was so quiet, no one even knew I was in the room. I think Hendricks even tried to nail me once, but I shocked him with the correct answer and didn't even try to make a joke.

WHEN I GOT HOME after school, I was surprised to see my dad's car already in the garage.

He was working on his old wooden speedboat. He bought it about five years ago, and it was totally trashed. It sat out in the backyard for a couple of years, but then he finally brought it into the garage and started working on it.

When Dad started to go to school at night, he stopped working on the boat.

"How come you're home so early?" I asked, walking into the garage. His hands were all oily and he was digging around in back by the motor.

"Hey, Mitchie," he said. "Hand me that ratchet."
I handed it to him.

"I took the afternoon off," he said, his face stuck deep inside the motor. "I finished that class late last night, and I didn't feel well, so I just came home." He pulled his head up and looked at me. "I tried to take a nap, but I couldn't sleep, so I thought I'd come out here and clean up a couple of things."

"Aren't you cold?" I asked.

"Yeah," he said. "I'm freezing, but I've only been out here for a few minutes. I just wanted to pull this part off so I could work on it inside." He yanked for a minute and finally pulled off some black metal mess. "Got it . . . So you survived detention, huh?"

"Yep," I said.

"And you're back in math?"

"Yeah. I think things are okay."

"They'd better be," he said. "I'm really sick of all the nonsense."

I leaned against the snowblower handle. "Believe it or not, Dad, so am I."

We didn't talk for a few minutes. I think both of us were trying to think of something to say. Then he wiped his hands off on a rag and looked at me.

"Mom liked what you did last night," he said. "She said you even cleaned up the kitchen and did all the dishes. That was very thoughtful."

"Well, Annie did all the hard stuff."

"Yeah," he replied. "But at least you thought of it. Maybe you're growing up a little bit."

"Dad?" I asked. "How come you went back to college?"

"Why, are you writing a book?"

"No," I answered. "I just don't see why anyone would want to go back to school when he doesn't have to. I mean, you've been doing it now for like two years—"

"It's only been a year and a half," he corrected. "And I've got about a year left."

"Okay," I said. "But it's real hard, isn't it?"

"It's not easy."

"So why are you doing it? It can't be fun."

"No, Mitchie, it's certainly not fun. But it's for a good cause. If I get my master's, I can probably move into something I like a little more. Make some more money. Get better set for our future. All the basic stuff. Why are you so interested in my education all of a sudden?"

"No reason, really," I said. "It's just that you're doing all this, and I never asked you why. It seems like something I ought to know. I mean, a guy should know why his dad is doing something important."

"Well," he said. "Now you know."

It was quiet again for a few minutes. And then I spoke up.

"Dad," I started, looking down at my boots. "I was a real jerk last week."

"Yes, you were," he agreed.

"In fact, I've had a pretty lousy fall."

"That's for sure."

This didn't seem to be going well. But then he said something else.

"Remember, Mitchie, you're thirteen. Most thirteen-year-old guys are jerks. But you're gonna be fourteen pretty soon, so you won't have any excuses anymore."

"I didn't mean what I said last week," I said. "You know that, right?"

"Yeah, I know," he answered, fiddling with the gooey boat part.

"I mean, I'm sure you said stuff like that to your dad."

"Well, that's where you're wrong, Mitchie. I never talked that way to my dad. Never. He would've knocked me across the room if I did."

From pictures I'd seen, my grandpa looked pretty tough, even though he wasn't very big.

"Did he ever smack you?" I asked.

"A couple of times," he said. "But only if I deserved it. It was nothing big."

"You've never smacked me."

"I've thought about it," he said. He put the oily part down and stretched his arms.

"Do you remember about a month ago when you kind of coasted in that game against Hastings?" he asked.

"Yeah, I guess so." It wasn't one of my fondest memories.

"The next day, I asked you why I should take time off work to race across town just to watch you play at half speed. You had a great answer, remember?"

I dropped my eyes to the floor. "Not exactly," I said.

"You told me not to come if I didn't want to watch."

There was silence for a second.

"Mitchie," he said. "That just about killed me. There is nothing I like better in the whole world than watching you, your brother, and your sister, and you practically told me not to bother. That was just so hard for me to understand. My dad thought sports were a waste of time. He never saw one of my games. I hated that. I couldn't figure him out."

"You and your dad didn't get along?" I asked.

"Basically, Mitchie, I was afraid of my dad. I don't mean I was afraid he was going to hurt me or anything. I was just afraid of him. I was afraid he thought I wasn't tough enough, or that I wasn't working hard enough. He was a very tough guy to please.

"But I've never wanted you guys to be scared of me. I want you to be able to talk to me and tell me what's going on. So when you went nuts on me last week, I figured that was just part of the deal. I didn't like it, but at least you weren't afraid to tell me what was on your mind. I even told your mom that for the first time all fall, I felt like you and me were making some progress."

"So you weren't mad?" I asked.

"Sure I was, at the time," he said. "Let's face it, Mitchie, you can be really pigheaded sometimes. But I don't mind a little yelling. You've heard your mother and me yell at each other, probably more lately because we've been so busy. But yelling doesn't bother me all that much. As long as you're honest with me. And maybe what you said made me think a little."

He paused again.

"You know," he went on, "I'm really proud of Chuck. But I'm proud of you too—most of the time. I think you've just had a rough fall."

"Yeah," I said. "I've been in a slump."

He smiled and slapped me lightly across the chin. "Well, snap out of it!" he said. Then he reached out and grabbed me around the shoulders.

He squeezed me tight, and I squeezed him back. "Like I said, I don't mind a little yelling," he said quietly in my ear. "But I like this a lot better."

"Me too," I said, trying to work myself free. "But you smell."

He laughed.

Then he squeezed me even tighter.

16

I DECIDED TO GET OUT of bed early the next morning and beat Sammy at his own game. If he was gonna leave his house early, I'd just leave mine a little earlier.

Of course, it was cold again, but not as cold as it had been. And it felt different outside. It was still dark, but there was no wind, and that made it even quieter than normal. It kind of felt like it does sometimes in the summer, right before a big rainstorm.

I dribbled a pinecone down the sidewalk, tapping it back and forth between my feet. My backpack flopped up and down with each step. If I was really going to be serious about playing varsity soccer, I figured I might as well start practicing right away. In Colombia and Brazil and joints like that, guys practice by kicking around oranges and stuff. Well, we don't have oranges falling from the trees in Minnesota.

We have pinecones.

As I dribbled down the path to Sam's house, I was thinking that I had just been through the longest fall in the history of the world. Summer seemed about four years ago. Snow seemed like something that had happened even a longer time ago, back when things were normal. Back when I was a kid—before everything changed.

But I had a feeling that things were going to pick up. At least now I had a plan. Dribbling this pinecone was just one small step in my triumphant comeback.

I'd already decided I wasn't going to knock on Sam's door. I would just lie low and wait for him to come out. For all I knew, his mom was covering for him and he was actually there the other times I'd stopped at the door. Heck, he could have had the whole neighborhood in on the plot.

I decided to lean against his neighbor's fence and wait. Even though I hadn't gotten cold walking over there, I was starting to lose feeling in my nose.

After about ten minutes or so, there was some action coming out of Sammy's garage. The door opened, and out came Sammy, his goofy tasseled hat falling off the side of his head.

I waited, letting him get a couple of houses down. I figured that way, he'd be too far from his house to go and run back in the door.

Silently, like a ninja warrior—a frozen ninja—I moved up alongside him. I was prepared to give him a heart attack.

But that's not what happened. My sudden appearance didn't faze him. It was like he was expecting me all the time.

"Hey, Mitchie," Sammy said, without slowing down or even looking at me. "I heard you were out of prison. What was it, parole? Or is this just some kind of work-release deal?"

"No, Sammy," I said. "They sprang me for good behavior on Monday. I even got to go back to math yesterday. They said if I stay out of trouble, I may get to vote someday."

"Thank you for the update." He didn't sound enthused.

"But there's more," I said. "Later today I'm leaving for Wyoming, where I'm gonna begin training for my new career as a rodeo clown."

"A rodeo clown, huh?" Sammy said, without any interest at all.

"Yeah," I told him. "There's big money in it. For a while I thought about going to Louisiana and being a roustabout on an offshore oil rig, but I decided to go the clown route instead."

"I don't even know what a roustabout is," Sammy said, still walking hard, his head down.

"Neither do I," I admitted. "That's why I decided to go the clown route."

"You're definitely clown material, Mitchie," he said.

"That I am, Sammy. That I am."

"When do you leave?" he asked.

"I think I'm gonna jump on one of those freight trains heading west later today. I have to sell some blood first to raise some traveling cash."

"Well," he said, "you've always got things figured out."

"That's me, Sammy. I'm a great planner."

We kept on walking, not saying anything for a while. Finally I broke the silence.

"Yep, 'Mitchie Evers, professional rodeo clown.' I like the way that sounds."

"Yeah," he said. "It sounds great. It sounds perfect, actually."

"I know it's glamorous, Sammy, but there's one thing holding me back."

"And that is?"

"I'm worried about you, Sammy," I said. "I'm deeply worried about you."

"Thanks," he said. "But somehow I'll manage."

"Sammy, I would give it up for you, you know," I said. "I'd just totally blow off my dream to be a rodeo clown. Just like that. All you have to do is ask."

"I'm not asking," Sammy said. "I don't think I could sleep nights knowing I ruined what could be a glorious career as a rodeo clown."

"But you *want* to ask."

He stopped dead in his tracks. We were about a half block from school.

"No, I don't, Mitchie," he said. "I think you could use a long train ride."

I decided it was time to get a little serious.

"Look, Sammy," I said. "You're killing me here. Let's just cut right to it. Here's how it always works. I do something stupid and you get real mad at me. You blow me off for a while and then everything's okay."

"Well, everything's not okay this time," he said.

"I know that," I said. "I'm telling you right now—and you know this is like the hardest thing I've ever done—but here it is . . . *I'm sorry*. I'm sorry for running you into the tree. I'm sorry about being a jerk. I'm sorry about all the other stupid stuff I've ever done in my whole stinking life."

I reached out and grabbed his arm.

"Sammy, I'm just plain sorry, okay?"

He was looking at his feet the whole time, kind of restless, rocking back and forth. Then he looked up at me.

"What, did you get religion or something?"

I didn't have an answer.

He kicked at the sidewalk, started to say something, then just turned and walked away, leaving me standing there like a geek.

I didn't know what to do.

Finally I called out to him.

"Well, should I get on that train, or what?"

He stopped, shook his head, and flung his hands in the air.

"No," he said eventually. "Don't get on the stinking train." He paused for what seemed like a week. Then he spoke again, but this time much more quietly. "Just stay here and continue to annoy me."

I smiled, because I knew I had him. Then he yelled back at me again.

"But don't bug me for a couple days," he said. "At least give me that."

"Sure thing, Sammy," I said. "I'll leave you alone until Saturday. I'll give you a break."

He turned and walked toward the school. I yelled at him again.

"Hey, Sammy," I yelled. "Did I tell you I'm gonna make the varsity soccer team next year?"

He spun around and yelled back. "What a coincidence," he said. "I'm gonna be the Vikings' starting quarterback next fall."

With that, he ducked into the building.

I'd give Sammy until Saturday. In fact, I would have given him anything he wanted. It was no fun not having a best friend.

17

NOW THAT I'D MADE some progress with my mom and dad and Sammy, I knew I had to fix things with Shea.

After dinner that night, I popped into her room. She had all her *Cool Planet* action figures lined up along her doll castle like they were about to storm the joint.

"You know," I said, "they don't have a castle on *Cool Planet*."

"Mitchie, you're so stupid," she said. "This is *not* a castle. It's the intergalactic squadron headquarters. And you can't come in here. I'm still mad at you."

"No you're not," I said. "You're just working me. Don't forget, you little bandit, I taught you all the tricks."

"I'm serious, Mitchie," she answered, not looking up. "I'm still mad at you. If you don't leave, I'll call Chuck in here and he'll knock you all over the place."

"Oh, c'mon. Like Chuck really scares me."

"It's gonna take more than just a spaghetti dinner—that Annie made—for me to forget how mean you were to me."

"Okay, we're making some progress here," I said.

"At least we're talking about what it's gonna take. So, Shea, tell me, what *is* it gonna take?"

She paused for moment, dropped one of her *Cool Planet* guys, and looked at me.

"You got five bucks?"

I reached into my pocket and pulled out a wrinkled-up bill.

"I've got one buck," I said.

"Give it to me," she demanded.

I handed it to her, and she jammed it into the big pocket in the front of her overalls.

"What else?" I asked.

"Well . . . there is one thing. But you'll never do it, because you're the meanest brother in the whole world."

I rolled my eyes, but I knew things were moving forward.

"Okay, what is it?" I asked.

"Forget it," she said. "You'll never do it."

I started to leave. "Have it your way."

"Wait," she said. "I'll tell you, but you'll just say no."

"Okay," I said, heading for the door.

"I want you to take me to a movie on Saturday."

I stopped and walked back toward her.

"Is that all?" I asked. "You're easy."

"You're not gonna like the movie."

"What?"

"You have to take me to see *Secret Princess*."

I collapsed onto her bed.

"Geez, not that lame girly movie about the doll and the fairies and princesses and stuff?"

"And you have to take Ali, too."

"Ali?" I shrieked. "She's a nutcase. She always spills her pop. And she has to go to the bathroom every five minutes."

"One more thing," Shea said. "You have to buy us some frozen yogurt after the movie."

"Anything else?" I asked. "Maybe you want me to rent a helicopter and fly you there?"

"Don't be stupid," she said. "You know Ali hates to fly. Anyway, that's the deal. You take me and Ali to see *Secret Princess* on Saturday and then buy us frozen yogurt, or I'll stay mad at you for the rest of my life. In fact, I can still hear many of those awful things you said to me. You know, Mitchie, you may have caused permanent damage. If you don't take me and Ali to this movie, I'll be so upset, I may have to be put into a mental hospital."

"Okay, stop," I said. "I'll take you and your goofy friend to the movie. But please, tell her not to wear those stupid sunglasses of hers. You know, the ones with the dolphins and the fish jumping all over the place."

Shea wrinkled her nose. "I gave her those sunglasses," she said. "For her birthday. They're cool."

I got up to leave.

"Can I at least get my buck back?" I asked.

"No chance," she said without looking up from her castle.

18

I FELT LIKE I WAS ON a roll, so I started to seri-
ously consider the idea of talking to Chuck.

It really shouldn't have been that hard to do. We
used to talk about everything.

Now it seemed like we went weeks without saying
a word to each other.

I don't know how that happened.

When I was little, I thought Chuck Evers was the
coolest guy in the whole world. I wanted to walk like
him, talk like him, look like him. I wanted to play the
same sports and read the same books. I couldn't wait
to grow into his old clothes.

And he was always great to me. He'd let me hang
out when his friends came over. He'd even let me go
up to the hockey rink with him, and if the teams
weren't even, he'd talk his buddies into letting me
play. That's how I got to be one of the truly great
outdoor hockey players.

I remember once when I was about ten, we were
up at Echo Park and it was the most perfect day to
play hockey. It was about twenty degrees and sunny.
They had just flooded the ice, so it was like glass.

Every time I touched the puck, I either scored a

goal or set one up. Of course, I did a little celebrating after every goal. And the boneheads on the other team didn't like that much.

They had this one goon on the team who could barely stand up on his skates, but he was dressed like he just walked out of a sporting goods store, with all the pads and gloves and stuff. He was about Chuck's age, and I could tell they knew each other. This guy must've been a little tired of me going around him and scoring all the time, because once when I came down the ice with the puck, he decided not to try and make a play. Instead, he just hammered me.

I was going to go to his right, but just as I started to make my move, he leaned forward with his knee up. He was about a foot taller than me, and he caught me right in the chest. I thought he was gonna just smack me and move on, which happens all the time. But instead, he kept driving me into the boards and then he fell on top of me. The shaft of his stick caught me across my nose. I fell back and banged my head on the ice. I could taste the blood running from my nose, into my mouth.

I thought I was dead.

Then all of a sudden, the guy popped off me—just like he was snapped up by a giant bungee cord. Chuck had him by his jersey, and his buddies were around him in semicircle.

Chuck just stood there, holding the guy against the boards and staring right into his eyes.

Then he spoke quietly.

"That must've been an accident, huh, Brian?"

asked Chuck. "Because I can't believe you'd be stupid enough to try and grind my brother into the boards with all of us standing here."

Chuck shook the guy and then spoke softly again. "That would be really foolish, wouldn't it, Brian?"

Chuck let him go, and the guy picked up his gloves and stick and, without saying a word, started skating toward the warming house.

BUT IT HAD BEEN a long time since anything like that happened. Chuck and I didn't even toss the football around together anymore.

Somewhere along the line, everything changed. One of those changes was Susan.

Instead of coming home and telling me about how he beat two midfielders and a defender to score the winning goal, these days he'd call her.

Instead of taking me to the mall, he'd take her.

Instead of asking me and Shea if we wanted to get something to eat when he felt like driving Dad's car, he'd go pick her up.

It was like he was disappearing.

When Chuck was eleven, he got real sick with some kind of virus. It wasn't like he was going to die or anything, but he felt horrible all the time. Nothing they tried ever worked, and he just wasn't getting better.

One day, they came home from the doctor and I heard my mom tell my dad that if this new medicine didn't work, they were going to have to put Chuck in the hospital to figure out what was wrong.

I was only eight, and I didn't hear everything. I only heard the part about Chuck going to the hospital and it scared the bejeezus out of me. I ran downstairs crying, with big tears bouncing off my lips. "Don't let Chuck go to the hospital," I cried. "Don't take him there!"

My dad picked me up and squeezed me.

I wiped my eyes and looked up at my dad. "He can't go to the hospital, Dad, because if he does, he'll never come home again."

"Don't worry," my dad said. "Chuck's not going anywhere. He's gonna be right here." I finally stopped crying, and Chuck never did have to go to the hospital.

But I was pretty sure that Chuck wasn't "right here" anymore. He wasn't going to be there to pull the bad guys off me at the rink anymore.

And what bothered me the most now was that the one thing that was gonna put us back together—the one thing I knew would make us tighter than we had ever been before—had just about slipped away.

And if I didn't move quick, that whole dream was shot.

AFTER PACING FOR about fifteen minutes, I finally got up the nerve to go talk to him.

From the hallway, I could hear Chuck's keyboard clicking in his room.

I was so stinking nervous, I decided to start with some comedy. Before I went in, I yelled from the hall.

"Come on, Chuck, put some pants on! You

shouldn't be sitting there in front of the window in your underwear."

Then I heard something unusual. It was a weird kind of laugh. It wasn't Chuck's laugh. It was different, a kind of wimpy girl laugh.

"Is that what you do, Chuck?" asked Susan as I walked into the room. They were both sitting at his desk, working very hard on something. "You sit around here and work in your underwear?" She laughed again.

I felt like a total idiot.

"Uh, hi, Susan," I said, finally finding my tongue. "I didn't know you were here."

"Obviously," said Chuck, not looking up from the screen.

"Hi, Mitchie," said Susan, leaning back and stretching. "I'm just helping your brother on a paper."

I put on my stunned look. "You must be confused, Susan. Chuck does not get help. He *gives* help."

"Not when it comes to English, Mitchie," she said. "When it comes to writing a simple paper, your big brother here is a serious bonehead."

"Finally," I said. "You mean there's something he's not perfect at?"

She twisted her face. "Mitchie, I don't think you know your brother as well as you think you do."

She got up and looked over Chuck's shoulder. I was kind of starting to see why Chuck liked hanging around with her. I mean, she wasn't exactly ugly.

"Well," I said. "You guys look really busy, so I'll just go back to the dungeon and play with the rats."

"No, you stay," said Susan. "I told Shea I'd go over and see her intergalactic squadron headquarters, whatever that is."

"Don't let her fool you," I warned Susan. "It's just a lame old doll castle."

"Whatever," she said, walking out of the room.

"What's up?" asked Chuck.

"Oh," I said. "I don't want to bother you. I didn't know Susan was over. I wouldn't want to, uh, *interrupt* anything."

He looked up. "Mitchie, don't be an idiot. What do you want?"

"No, really," I said. "I gotta ask you about something important, and I don't want Susan to distract you." I winked. "Know what I mean?"

In like a lightning motion, he flipped his pencil at me, hard, and nailed me right smack in the forehead.

"Hey! You could've taken my eye out!"

He shrugged. "Yeah, you're right. I could have. But I chose not to."

He leaned back in his chair and rubbed his forehead.

"You know, Mitchie," he said, "I hate this English junk. How come you never have any trouble with it?"

I walked over and sat on the bed. "Because even though people don't realize it, I'm actually the brilliant one in this family. And unlike you, I read a book once in a while."

"Who has time to read?" he asked.

"Well, when you're out there all the time trying to save the world, I guess it's hard to fit reading in. See, Chuck, I've told you before. You gotta stop and smell the roses."

"Yeah, yeah," he said. "So what'd ya want?"

I paused for a moment. This was it. I just sat there for a second. I didn't know exactly how to start, and he could see that.

"Well?" he asked.

I tried to pull myself together. "If I ask you a real question," I said, "will you give me a real answer?"

He raised his eyes. "What's going on, Mitchie, some girl look at you funny in the lunch line?"

I didn't even have a comeback. "No, I'm serious," I said. "This is important."

He could tell I meant it. "Okay, okay," he said. "I'm listening."

I looked down and kind of shuffled my feet. I'd been planning this conversation for a long time, but I still didn't feel ready. "I don't know how to ask this, so I'm just gonna ask. Do you think I have any chance at all of making varsity next year?"

"In what?" he asked.

"In checkers," I said. "Quit being a jerk. You know what I'm talking about." I asked him again. "Can I make the varsity soccer team next year as a ninth-grader?"

He looked totally surprised.

"Geez, Mitchie, I don't know." He stopped for a

second, then spoke again. "If you quit halfway through the season, I'm guessing it will be *real* hard."

I was expecting that.

"All right," I said. "But forget about that for now. What if I work real hard, starting tomorrow—harder than anyone in the whole world? What if I have a great summer season and come into practice next fall all pumped up? I mean, what if I do everything right and keep my mouth shut and do all the things you did? What if I don't screw around and I listen to the coach?"

Chuck ran his fingers through his hair.

"I don't know," he said.

He saw the disappointment in my face.

"Hey, Mitchie," he said. "I'm not trying to be a jerk here. But we've got a good young team coming back and we're not losing a lot of guys. And face it, you didn't help yourself by quitting this year."

"I know, I know," I said. "But are you telling me I have *no* chance?"

"No, I'm not saying that. But to be honest, I think it's a real long shot."

I tried hard to stop it, but I think Chuck could see my eyes starting to get a little red. And the look on his face changed.

"Look, Mitchie, when I made varsity as a freshman, we had a horrible team. I played varsity, but we were like three and eighteen that year. We were awful. I bet if you had been a freshman that year, you could've played varsity too.

"But next year, we're gonna be loaded. We should be the best team in the conference. I think for the first time in five years we might not have *any* freshmen make varsity. Heck, we only had one make it this year. You know, Mitchie, when I made it, three other freshmen did too."

He was trying, but he wasn't making me feel any better.

"Maybe I'm wrong," he said, getting up and walking over to the bed. "Maybe you can surprise me."

"Is it just that I quit?"

"No, it's not just that you quit—even though that was a really stupid thing to do."

I jumped off the bed. "That's not what I meant. I meant . . . am I good enough?"

He thought about that.

"The thing is, Mitchie, being good isn't the whole answer. Sometimes you also gotta be a good suck-up."

"Wow," I thought. "Chuck Evers is admitting he's a good suck-up."

Then he caught himself. "Forget that," he said. "That's not what I mean. What I mean is, you have to have the right attitude. I worked my butt off freshman year. I did everything the coaches wanted. I was the first guy on the field and the last guy to leave. I was always first in line for drills. I even helped pick up the equipment. I was the perfect team player."

"What if *I* did that?"

"But that's not you, Mitchie. I did it because I knew I had to. I wasn't a natural like you—"

A *natural?*

"I had to work like a stinking Marine. Otherwise I didn't think I was going to make it. And you know what? It wasn't any fun. I mean, I made the team, but the rest of the guys thought I was a geek because I worked so hard."

"That's just you, Chuck."

"But it's not you," he shot back. "See, Mitchie, you're different. I love to watch you play because you're out there laughing and joking. You have so much fun when you play. I can't see you being serious enough next year to make the coaches happy."

"But I can do it," I said.

"Maybe," he answered. "But do you want to? Do you really want to? I mean, what's the big deal? Go out next year, work hard, have some fun. Make the coaches forget about what you did this year. You'll make it as a sophomore. That's still real good."

"But I want to make it *next* year," I said as forcefully as I could.

"What's so incredibly important about next year?"

"Because," I said finally, "I want to play with *you.*"

He sat there for a moment, speechless.

"Geez," he said. "I guess I never even thought about that. But you have been, huh?"

I wiped my eye and looked at him.

"I've been thinking about it since the day you made it as a ninth-grader," I said, slowly pacing the room, squeezing my hands. "It all clicked. Your senior year and my freshman year. Think about it. We've played hockey and football and soccer together since I could walk. But we've never been on a real team to-gether. So I figured this would be perfect. It's the last chance we could ever do this.''

Chuck still looked confused.

"Okay, but if you wanted to make varsity as a ninth-grader so bad,'' he asked, "why did you quit this year? You had to know that was gonna mess things up, right?''

"Yeah,'' I said. "But that was later. At first I thought it was gonna be easy. You made it as a fresh-man, so I would too. That's only natural, right? But then you became like this soccer star, this incredible goal-scoring machine, and I knew I wasn't as good as you. And if I wasn't as good as you, I wouldn't make it as a freshman. And if I didn't make it as a freshman, we'd *never* play on the same team.''

I went on. "But Hendricks wrecked everything. He moved me to forward. I didn't want to play forward. That's where *you* play. Midfield was my spot. I owned it. I was the first Evers to play there. Nobody could say, 'Well, Mitchie, you don't score like your brother.' Well, duh, as a midfielder I don't have to even try. I play a different kind of game back there.''

I stopped for a second, and then went on.

"It just never worked. When Hendricks knocked me down to the third line, I thought, 'I may as well just quit.' ''

Chuck smiled. "That's brilliant thinking,'' he said.

"Yeah, well, you know me,'' I said. "I'm a stinking genius.''

We sat there for a few seconds and didn't say a

thing. Chuck lay down on his bed and kicked off his shoes.

"So you and me playing varsity together, huh?" he asked. "On the same team?"

"That was the plan."

"Mom and Dad would love that, wouldn't they?"

"Yeah, I guess they would."

"You know," Chuck said, "you might actually have to get in shape for once in your life—real shape. In the Lake Conference, you have to run your butt off. The coaches are gonna make it real hard on you, too. And think about it, I'm a captain. I'll lean on you big-time, especially if you give me any lip."

I threw my hands up.

"I know all that," I said. "But do you think I can do it?"

"Honest?"

"Yeah," I said. "Honest."

"No," he said. "I don't think you can."

I sighed real deep.

"But wait," he said. "I'm not the coach. Prove me wrong. I mean, what's the worst thing that can happen? You work your butt off. Your game gets better. You finally get in real shape. And maybe a miracle will happen. Maybe half the team will come down with hepatitis or something and we'll need you."

He saw my jaw tighten and my eyes flash.

"Relax," he continued. "You can run with me and work out with me. I'll help you every way I can. You give it your best shot, and maybe it'll work out. Maybe we'll be playing together in the state tourney.

That would be great. But if that doesn't happen, that's okay too. Because you'll be a better player. You'll be way ahead of where you are right now.''

"Why would you even want to help me?" I asked. "I mean, I never even said anything to you after you set the scoring record."

"It's simple. I'm afraid that if I don't help you, you'll end up in some alley somewhere," he said. "Then I'd be forced to take you in and I'd be stuck with you the rest of my life. I think I'll have it easier this way."

Just then Susan appeared.

"Have you guys seen Shea's setup?" she asked with a huge grin. "It's incredible. I swear, she's going to be a director someday. It's like a huge movie set, with all kinds of characters and costumes. It's amazing."

"I'll go see it in a few minutes," said Chuck. "Mitchie here was just telling me how he's gonna make varsity next year and make my life miserable."

I gave him my tough-guy look—my pretend tough-guy look—and started heading for the door. But as I passed his desk, he grabbed me by the arm and pulled me around so we were looking straight into each other's eyes.

We stared at each other for a second. Then he spoke, quietly and directly.

"You know, Mitchie," he said, letting go of my arm but still staring right at me. "It would be pretty great. It would be pretty stinking great. I mean that."

"I know," I said, my voice cracking. I headed for the door.

When I got to the hall, I stopped for a second and kind of leaned against the wall. I was exhausted. Then I heard Susan ask Chuck if he thought I had a chance.

"He's good," I heard him answer. "But it's gonna be *so* hard. Still, he might surprise me."

There was silence for a second. And then I heard him again.

"He's a little wise guy—but believe me, Susan, he can flat-out *play*."

19

THAT NIGHT I HAD that dream again, the same one I'd been having for a month. But this time it was a little different.

The dream was about missing a game. This time I was still looking for my team, but I wasn't panicking. Somehow I knew I'd find them.

Then—again—when I was dead asleep, a shot of light pierced my brain.

It was Shea rolling back my left eyelid.

"Mitchie!" she yelled in my ear. "Get up, get up!"

I sprang up and tried to jump out of my sheets, thinking the house was on fire. I got tangled in my bedspread, twisted my right knee, and fell flat on my face, just barely getting a forearm down to break my fall.

"Quit messing around, Mitchie!" said Shea. "You need to get dressed!"

"What's going on?" I finally got out. "Are we burning down?"

"Just get dressed!"

By the huge smile on her face, I could tell there was no tragedy, so I slowed down a bit and sat back on the edge of my bed. It wasn't till then that I noticed that Shea looked like she had just stepped in from Alaska. She was wearing her big parka and snowpants, along with the old ski hat that I'd given her last year. The scarf from Grandma was wrapped all around her neck, and on her feet were her brand-new boots, the ones she couldn't wait to wear.

Then I figured it out.

I got untangled, jumped to my feet, and headed for my window.

Outside was a whole new world, white and clean and crisp.

"How much did we get?" I asked.

"The TV said seven inches," answered Shea. "It's been snowing all night."

I threw on the sweatpants that I'd dropped on the floor the night before and then went into my closet and found another pair to put over them. I pulled on some thick socks and slipped a stretched-out turtleneck over my T-shirt.

We ran downstairs and I got so far ahead of myself, I nearly ran over Shea. As I pulled on my big Arctic boots, Shea tossed some hats and mittens out of the hall closet.

"No," I shouted as I zipped up my big down jacket. "Get me those big leather choppers that Dad wears when he shovels." She found them and threw them at me.

We stepped out from the laundry room and opened the garage door. Snow had drifted up about two to three feet in front of the door, and Shea ran from the back of the garage right into the middle of the biggest drift. She nearly disappeared.

There is something very special about unbroken snow, and we waded through it slowly and carefully. We had to squint at first because the sun's glare off the snow was so bright, but after a few feet we were okay. It had to be only around ten degrees above zero, but there was no wind, so we weren't cold.

It was still early, and as we walked, the only marks in the snow were two skinny tire tracks, probably from the guy delivering the newspapers.

It was the best kind of snow, soft under our feet as we walked, falling powdery off our boots. This wasn't the kind of sloppy snow that usually comes down in early November, the kind that melts as it hits the ground, turning gray and mucky from the salt and the dirt in the street. I had waited for this snow, and it was worth the wait.

When we got to the park, it was like no one else had ever been there before, like we were explorers who had just discovered this whole new place. With the thick layer of snow, the lake seemed to go on forever, and the ice-fishing houses out in the middle looked like some kind of magical troll village.

I looked out from the edge of the lake, reaching down every once in a while to grab a handful of snow and stuff it in my mouth. I looked over and saw Shea on her back making snow angels, then turned and looked out again into the great, vast whiteness.

I just stood there trying to suck it all in, trying to forget about what the world even looked like before this very moment, before the snow came and turned everything white.

Then, *bam!*

Out of nowhere, someone reached from behind and smacked a whole handful of snow in my face. I knew it wasn't Shea because she was still rolling around like a pig in mud.

I jumped and tried to shake it off, but a bunch of snow still slid down my shirt, freezing all the way. As I stomped and screamed, I turned to see Chuck laughing his lame head off, totally thrilled that he'd been able to sneak up on me and wash my face in the snow.

"Pretty funny, geek boy," I shouted as I put my head down and rammed him at full speed, sending him flying backward into the snow.

"What?" asked Chuck looking up, his eyes wide. "You still can't handle your big brother?"

I jumped on him and he tried to push me off, and we wrestled there until Shea jumped on top, dumping snow on both of us. Chuck couldn't stop laughing, and even though the cold, stinging snow was getting into my mittens, boots, and shirt, I couldn't stop either.

Finally I was able to roll away. I watched Shea do her pro wrestler routine on Chuck, and listened to my brother giggle like some wimpy girl. Way back in the distance I saw Annie walking toward us from Keller Lane.

And even though the snow burned as it made its way up my sleeves and down my neck, I started thinking that maybe this was exactly what I needed so I could finally wipe the slate clean and start fresh.

Maybe all I'd needed was some snow.